REFUGE

ZONE CYBORGS BOOK 5

JESSICA MARTING

SHADOW PRESS

REFUGE

Refuge (Zone Cyborgs #5)

ISBN 978-1-989780-18-3

Cover art by German Creative

CONTENT WARNING:

This book contains discussion of abuse.

For David, as always.

CHAPTER 1

"YOU'RE *sure* you want me to leave you here?" Cecily Barris, the *Gray Ghost*'s captain, stuck her head out of the ship's exterior door and made a face at the sight before her.

Rordan Alexander didn't tear his gaze from the darkened dry dock that stretched before the *Gray Ghost*'s open exterior door. Spaceport 44's recycled air seeped into the ship, smelling faintly of used cooking oil, human sweat, and the sickly sweet odor of darfin. The lights that still worked flickered overhead.

"Is there anyone even here?" Cecily asked incredulously.

Rordan finally spoke. "Of course. The air and gravity controls are clearly working."

"You could still go on to the Brava System with the rest of us," Cecily said. "You have enough money now to go anywhere in the galaxy if you want."

"What I want is to be here," Rordan replied. He finally turned to face her and her bewildered expression. "I appreciate your help in our big rescue, and I wish you the best as you start your new lives."

"Don't you want to say goodbye to the rest of your friends?" Cecily asked, referring to the rest of his surviving cyborg brothers-in-arms.

"We aren't really friends."

He didn't think it was possible for the mercenary captain to be shocked, but her widened eyes at his words proved otherwise. "All I've wanted since I was trapped on Omega-Three-Omega was to get my life back," Rordan explained. "That means I need to start here."

"On this piss-poor excuse for a space station?"

"Yes," he said firmly. "I don't expect you to understand that, but it's here."

"You're a cyborg," Cecily said as if he could ever forget that. "You're in a much more vulnerable position here. Three of your friends..." She caught herself and started again. "Three of your fellow cyborgs died tonight, and we don't know why."

Like he could forget that, either. The memory of Aaron Bell's body hitting the floor, completely out of nowhere, would always be fresh. He'd forever remember, in painstaking detail, thanks to his cybernetically enhanced brain, how the light in Aaron's eyes went out. Rordan thought he might have actually seen his soul leaving his body.

"I'll be fine," Rordan said. He slung his duffel over his shoulder, not that he had much in the way of physical possessions. "Thank you for your help, Captain Barris."

Without waiting for a reply, or bothering to check on the remaining cyborgs still aboard the *Gray Ghost*, Rordan walked down the ship's exterior ramp to Spaceport 44's dock, then turned a corner to a darkened corridor.

Ten months later

Kurkay-2's Westingtown settlement wasn't exactly the warm and balmy Princess Cay of Sidra Prime, but Dasha Caron wasn't about to complain about it. She missed the beaches and sunshine of her adopted hometown, but the settlement still had a great deal of charm.

And *rain*. At least it was light and rather refreshing, and there was usually a rainbow or two after a shower. She didn't think she could ever tire of the rainbows.

Dasha people-watched from the window seat in her living room, taking in the sight of Westingtown waking up and starting the day. Her third-floor apartment overlooked Westingtown's quaint downtown area, populated by Zone expats, refugees and some native Bravans who didn't mind Kurkay-2's near-constant rain.

She sipped her tea and watched as the couple who owned the mercantile across the street opened up the store for business. *I should take a shower and...*

What, exactly? She'd been a primary school teacher on Sidra Prime; since she and her father arrived on Kurkay-2 nearly two months prior, she hadn't done much or worked. She helped out her father, a doctor, when she could, but she wasn't a nurse or medic, and she hated the sight of blood. Her ability to help was limited.

She missed teaching children. She missed feeling useful.

You came here for adventure, remember?

Dasha turned away from the window as that memory popped back into her head. What an idiot she'd been, thinking she'd get to do fun and interesting things once she was away from her home. The most exciting thing to happen to her so far was being chased by an angry, jealous goat named Dolly, who hated everyone except Anders Barris, a new friend of hers who farmed nearby.

Anders was a cyborg. At least she could say she'd met cyborgs and maybe helped save a few of them.

That was a big "maybe." There was still a cyborg from Anders's circle, Rordan Alexander, who was unaccounted for, despite some of the best minds in the galaxy searching for him.

There was also the issue of cyborgs not officially existing, she couldn't very well tell anyone that she'd helped them out.

A knock at her door had her nearly dropping her teacup, and as it was, a little liquid sloshed on the floor and her pajama top. "Damn," she muttered, setting the cup aside. No one had messaged her, asking to visit. She hoped it wasn't an emergency.

Her apartment's ident verification system was offline, but even if it had worked, it would've been useless. Subcutaneous ident chips weren't in wide use in the Brava System as its government didn't make a habit of spying on its citizens like the Zone. Dasha wasn't especially worried about her safety here, but she was still cautious. "Hello?" she said through the door's comm unit. "Who is it?"

She heard a male throat being cleared. "Delivery for Miss Dasha Caron."

Dasha's senses immediately went on high alert, and she cursed herself for not keeping her spanner within reach. The small hand weapons weren't strictly legal on Kurkay-2, but it wasn't like she advertised she owned one. "I didn't order anything," she said.

"I don't know anything about that," the man said. "I just have a delivery for Miss Dasha Caron."

"Who from?"

He let out an exasperated sigh. "Look, lady, could you just get your package? Yours isn't the only delivery I have today."

Delivery services were rare in Westingtown, the community being so small that its residents could find whatever they wanted within a fifteen-minute walk of their apartments. Unfortunately, the small size meant that there wasn't much in the way of law enforcement at the moment.

Stars damn it all. "Just a minute," Dasha said, looking down at her tea-stained pajamas. She quickly raced through her apartment until she found her spanner, hidden under a corner of her mattress. She tucked it behind her pajama waistband and steeled herself, then opened the door.

A nondescript man, a few centimeters taller than her, stood in front of her apartment door, irritation across his features and his hands empty. She knew immediately that she made a terrible mistake. "Dasha Caron?" he said.

"Yes?"

He lunged at her, but she stepped out of the way, and he crashed into the foyer before she could further react.

It took a few seconds for her brain to process what was happening, that someone had forced his way into her apartment. He reached for her again, and she snapped into action, moving away from him, but still too shocked to scream.

"Where's your father?" he snarled.

Her father's warnings over the years clanged through her mind. *Dad always said this could happen.* "Are you a cyborg?" she asked, hating the quiver in her voice.

"No, of course not." He gave her a look that clearly questioned her intelligence. "But I'm looking for your father."

Dasha reached behind her for her spanner, hands shaking. "Who are you?"

"Doesn't matter."

Before she could mull it over, Dasha threw the spanner at him, hitting him square in the throat. He froze as the palm-sized weapon latched on to his body with tiny claws, dispersing a neurotoxin into his system. She froze, simultaneously horrified and grateful that the attempted attack was over.

Was that his carotid artery?

Could someone survive that?

But as the man crumpled to the floor, his breath stopped with a final death rattle, Dasha's question was answered.

Cecily Barris stood over the body, open loathing on her face as she regarded the dead man. Dasha didn't know what to make of that.

"Cecily?" Dasha said quietly. "I'm sorry to spring this on you, but you were the only person I could think of who might be able to help."

The former mercenary turned to face Dasha. "I'm glad you called me instead of Anders," she said. "Or anyone else, really." She regarded the body again. "It's so rude to just barge in like that when it's not even ten in the morning." Her lip curled in distaste. "Fucking Dalton."

The name meant nothing to Dasha, but she was surprised to hear Cecily say it. "You know him?"

"Yeah, he's not exactly discreet. Anyone involved in any part of the Zone's black market knows who Janek Dalton is, even if they haven't actually dealt with him directly." She lifted a dark eyebrow at Dasha. "You're awfully relaxed for someone who just killed a man. Are you *sure* you aren't a secret assassin?"

Dasha managed a tiny smile at the remark, remembering the first time they'd met, back at the treehouse she'd shared with her dad in Princess Cay. She'd had her spanner and an electromagnetic pulse device at the ready, just in case she had to defend herself against Cecily and her cyborg boyfriend, Jason Formosa. Cecily was amazed at Dasha's later revelation that she'd been armed for that meeting.

"I'm sure I'm not a secret assassin," she said. The protective shock of what she'd done was wearing off, and she was now dangerously close to tears. Blinking them back, she said, "If I hadn't opened the door, he probably would've gone on to find my father."

Cecily nodded. "Last I checked, your dad was still safe aboard the *Gray Ghost*, but I'll let him know what happened."

"Thank you." Dr. Caron eschewed living in Westingtown, preferring to stay on Cecily's ship, which was currently on her brother's farm. Her father needed to be around a working sickbay to care for their friend Serena, the only known female cyborg, during her pregnancy. He didn't want to attract attention to himself as long as the rogue cyborg was still at large.

Dasha remembered the missing cyborg when she thought of her father. "So, you know for sure this isn't Rordan Alexander?" she asked.

"He's too old to be Rordan, and I've met Dalton before anyway," Cecily pointed out. "Rordan's in his late twenties, like you. And again, I know Janek Dalton a hell of a lot better than Rordan. Dalton was the person who arranged the black market surgery for my first cybernetic heart."

In her panic over what she'd done, Dasha had forgotten that Cecily knew what the missing cyborg looked like.

"Dalton's an idiot anyway," Cecily said, sighing. She nudged him with her booted foot. "*Was* an idiot. Dasha, I'll get him out of here soon, and I'll find out who he was working for."

"Maybe Wilton Intergalactic Fluid Technology," Dasha said.

Cecily didn't look surprised to hear the name of the private water company based in the Zone. It was after black market cyborg technology, all the better to create a stockpile of workers who could be silenced and more easily controlled. "That makes sense," she said. "Wilton probably has bounties out for cyborgs and the tech needed to enhance people, which would explain why he was after your dad, and he was too dumb to think to look for him on my ship." She paused, considering her words for a few seconds. "Or smart. He knows what I'd do to him if I caught him near the *Ghost*."

"What are you going to do with him?" Dasha asked, trying to keep the conversation focused on the body lying on the floor. Tears pricked at her eyes. She wanted it gone, for this whole morning to have never happened.

"I'm thinking the easiest thing to do is load the body on whatever ship he used to get here, put it on autopilot, and set it to blow once it's cleared Kurkay-2's atmosphere," Cecily replied. "Well, the easiest thing to do would be to bury him on Anders's farm, but I don't think he'd be okay with that."

"Are you going to tell Anders and Valenna?"

"Yeah, but only because everyone we know has had to deal with Dalton at some point, and they'll be glad to know he's dead," Cecily said. "Valenna and her sister *really* hated him. But Anders definitely won't let me dispose of the body on his property." She pulled away enough so they could face each other. "Take a shower and get dressed. I'll get Jason, and we'll deal with Dalton, all right? No one's going to jail or anything."

Dasha hadn't even considered the possibility of jail. The very thought of it triggered a fresh wave of tears.

"Dash, it's really okay," Cecily said. "I promise. Everyone's always a little freaked out the first time they kill someone."

Dasha couldn't form a response to that.

"We need to find out how he got here," Cecily said. "We have to find out who hired him and what exactly he and his employer were after. Between everyone in our group of friends, we have the skill sets to do just that."

Dasha nodded, but Cecily's words did nothing to soften the impact of what she'd just done.

"Go," Cecily said, pointing to the hallway that led to her bathroom and bedroom. "Get washed up. You did a good thing today, I promise."

As she padded down the hallway, she thought about how

she had always craved adventure. She just wished she'd been more specific about what kind.

A couple of hours later, Dasha was sitting at Anders Barris and Valenna Merchant's kitchen table, an untouched cup of tea in front of her. Anders and Valenna sat opposite her and Cecily, and Cecily's boyfriend Jason leaned against the counter.

All wore grave expressions, and Dasha knew hers had to be the same. Even though she'd already been assured she'd done nothing wrong once they learned what happened, she couldn't shake the guilt that crept up every time she thought about the squelching sound her spanner made when it lodged itself in Janek Dalton's throat.

Valenna broke the silence. "Lukas and Cressida should be here soon."

Dasha had only met Valenna's sister and her partner a handful of times since they relocated to Kurkay-2, and her nervousness ticked up another notch. Lukas Best was the original cyborg, designed to be a living weapon in ways the other illegally enhanced hadn't been.

And some of them, including Rordan Alexander, had a fatal flaw deliberately embedded in them as a means of ensuring compliance, a kill switch in the brain. It was vital they find Rordan as soon as possible so Dasha's father could deactivate it.

"I didn't want to say too much over public transmit links, but they know something's up with Dalton," Valenna continued.

As if on cue, their farmhouse's door opened, and Cressida called, "Hello?"

Valenna immediately sprang out of her seat to greet them,

and Dasha heard murmurs and whispers from the foyer. A few seconds later, she heard Cressida exclaim, "Holy shit, really?"

Shortly after, Lukas said, "Good to hear."

But there wasn't a trace of delight to be found on their faces when they walked into the kitchen. "Hi," said Cressida, caution in her voice. "Are you okay, Dasha?"

Dasha pasted a smile on her face. "I'll be fine."

"The body's been disposed of?" Lukas said to Cecily by way of greeting. Cressida nudged him. To Dasha, Lukas said, "Sorry, I just want to make sure his death can't be traced to us."

"The body's on his ship," Cecily said. "I'm going to launch it after we've stripped it of all data and set it to blow up when it breaks the atmosphere. I need cyborg help for that." She looked between Jason and Lukas, both of whom had data ports built into them.

"Are you sure that's wise?" Lukas asked. "The Brava System isn't like the Zone. Accidents are investigated."

Jason nodded. "We were very lucky no one traced that Scout explosion back to us," he said to Cecily. "That was sheer dumb luck."

"Excuse me?" Cecily said. "I *do* know how to cover my tracks."

"And people don't need to do that as often here as they do in the Zone," Jason reminded her. "The authorities investigate when people die. The best thing to do to get rid of Dalton and his ship is to request authorization to depart from wherever he was docked at, launch the ship like usual, and hop on a shuttle before scuttling it in the Rims or somewhere else no one will care about."

"He's right," said Lukas. "This is going to be a group effort if we want to get away with it."

Cecily narrowed her eyes at both men, then looked at

Anders, who was watching their exchange in silence. "Well?" she asked. "Don't you have anything to add?"

"Not really," Anders said. "I'm just pleasantly surprised that it wasn't you who killed someone this time."

"This isn't the time to gloat," Cecily said, voice rising.

Before Anders could offer a rejoinder, Lukas said, "She's right. We have to get back to Dalton's ship and figure out what we're going to do with it. You're coming with us, Formosa?"

Jason nodded. "Have you ever downloaded a ship's complete specs into your head? Because we'll have to do that."

"No."

"It fucks you up a little. You'll be dizzy for a bit."

"I can live with that," Lukas replied. "Cecily, can you take us there?"

Cecily and Dasha both rose. "I'm coming with you," Dasha said. "I have to do this."

None of them, bless them, said a word otherwise.

She had to go, to see what information Dalton had about the surviving cyborgs and who hired him. And most importantly, who was after her father.

Janek Dalton's ship was a stripped-down freighter called the *Raider*, docked in a public shipyard a few kilometers outside Westingtown.

The ship's slatted metal deck was filthy, and every door was palm-coded. Dasha lingered in the cockpit's doorway as Jason and Lukas plugged themselves into the first ports they found and watched in morbid fascination as they downloaded everything they could about Dalton's mission into themselves. Their eyes flitted back and forth as they rapidly read everything, and Jason swayed a little in place.

She was so transfixed she jumped when Cecily spoke.

"Sorry," Cecily said. "I have Dalton here. I'm leaving him in the cockpit. Just in case his ship is investigated, so there's evidence of his remains here."

Dasha looked over Cecily's shoulder and blanched. She'd dragged the dead man by his feet, which stuck out from the blanket he was wrapped in. At least there wasn't any blood visible.

"Ugh," Dasha said and moved out of the doorway.

But she needed to do this, needed to see where this Dalton guy came from and find out why he was after her father.

Was she looking for closure? Or just making sure that she'd killed someone who might have deserved it? Because the stripped-down, creepy ship aside, she hadn't seen any evidence that he was evil.

Maybe he was just trying to survive in difficult conditions, like Cecily.

Good God, how could people live with themselves after they'd killed someone, even in self-defense?

Dasha waited in the corridor for the rest of them to finish up. She heard a thud as something fell to the deck, followed by a squelching noise and Cecily snarling, "Oh, God damn it. You'd think someone who didn't have any fucking brains in his head wouldn't be so squishy already."

Her stomach roiled. *I think I might puke.*

Breathing deeply, Dasha walked away, along the length of the corridor. Every door she passed had biometric locks and old-fashioned deadbolts on them, the sight of which sent shivers down her spine. When she tried a few doors at random, they didn't budge. Only one opened, and when Dasha looked inside, she saw it was a supply closet, full of sonicuffs, ion rope dispensers, and spanners more sophisticated than the one she'd used to kill Dalton.

Okay, there's *the confirmation you needed to know Dalton really was terrible.*

To her surprise, the door opposite the supply closet opened automatically at her presence, and when she stuck her head through it, she saw it was a stairwell. Cursing from the cockpit—Jason this time, as he helped Cecily wrangle the body—drifted down the corridor, reminding her she needed to get back to her friends.

But curiosity got the better of her, and she took her first steps down the stairs.

Why was she doing this to herself?

She already knew the answer: she'd never seen evil up close. She was sickly fascinated with what she was finding on the *Raider*, as much as she loathed its captain.

Another locked door greeted her at the foot of the stairs, the engine room, she guessed. But next to it, she found a bug-out room, complete with a single-occupancy escape pod and duffel full of clothes.

A rumbling under her feet and the roar of engines nearby had her snapping back to attention. "What the hell?" she said aloud, the words muffled, and dashed for the stairs.

It sounded like the *Raider* was readying for takeoff.

The door didn't automatically open for her this time. Dread had her hands shaking as she pounded on the door, then kicked it in frustration when it didn't budge. Finally, she spied an emergency handle in the door's top-left corner and tugged. It didn't move.

"God damn it!" she shouted over the engines. Putting every bit of strength she could into it, she pulled as hard as she could until the door opened just enough for her to wiggle through.

She ran up the corridor. "Cecily?"

If she answered, she couldn't hear them. *Why is it so bloody loud?*

"Jason? Lukas?"

She stuck her head in the cockpit and screamed. It was

empty, save for Dalton whose makeshift shroud had come loose. All Dasha could focus on was the wound on his throat that she'd caused.

"Automatic emergency takeoff initiating in twenty seconds," a comp voice announced. It sounded an awful lot like Janek Dalton's voice. "This is what happens when you try to steal my ship, you fuckers."

"What?" Dasha shrieked as if the voice could answer her.

She had twenty seconds to get off the *Raider* before it took off for God knew where.

The airlock! That must be where the others were. She retraced her steps until she got to the airlock accessway.

The exterior door was already shut and sealed. When she looked out its small, round viewport, she saw Cecily, Jason, and Lukas looking at the *Raider*, horrified expressions on their face. They just figured out Dasha was still onboard.

The absolute stupidity of what she'd done hit her full force, and she screamed, pounding her fists against the door like it would open under her strength.

"Run away!" she screamed at them. Even someone as inexperienced with spaceflight as Dasha knew how dangerous it could be to hang out at a launch site.

The *Raider* shuddered, and Dasha was thrown against the nearest wall as the ship lifted herself into the air and hurtled toward the atmosphere.

CHAPTER 2

THE TEMPLE WAS SILENT, and Brother Rordan's footsteps were muffled by the heavy slippers mandated by its resident monks. His blue novice robes glided behind him, trailing on the highly-polished floor. An occasional dust mote drifted in the air, highlighted by the moonlight streaming through the temple's windows.

He entered the silent prayer room. Blue and white-clad monks lined up on the floor, their knees resting on pillows whose covers matched their robes, everyone in quiet contemplation. Brother Rordan selected a white pillow from the pile in a big woven-reed basket and took the first available space he saw. He kneeled and closed his eyes, pushing out every distraction from his thoughts.

Not that there were many. His mind drifted back to the ground apple cake he'd enjoyed after dinner tonight, a rare and luxurious treat. He could go for another one right now if he was honest with himself.

And the twin moons were definitely pretty. *Thanks be to the stars and universe for creating them.*

He thought back to his Great Faith teaching master, back to the first lesson he had after arriving at the Order of the

Benevolent Stars: "Every prayer should begin with gratitude to the powers who keep us alive."

Brother Rordan repeated it to himself, this time with as much feeling as he could muster. *Thanks be to the stars and universe for Glissat's twin moons. They're beautiful, and I love the perpetual nighttime.*

Thanks be to you for my eyes that I get to enjoy their splendor the way they were designed to be.

A nagging thought tugged him away from his prayers. *Even though my eyes aren't like those of the rest of the brothers here, I still thank you for them.*

Brother Rordan's eyes weren't fully organic, and he didn't know what happened to them, nor did he care to know. If the stars and universe decided that he needed to know more about his life prior to joining the Order of the Benevolent Stars, they would grant him his old memories.

He breathed deeply in a fresh attempt to banish those thoughts away. It didn't matter what his old life was; all that mattered now was that he was here, learning in the presence of great men, and improving himself.

Thanks be to the stars and universe for the teachers here at the temple.

I humbly ask that I might be allowed to take my vows as soon as I can. I've been so patient and studied so much.

Brother Rordan opened his eyes and briefly glanced around the room at the other monks, their heads still bowed in prayer.

A memory flitted through his mind, breaking his concentration.

Stepping off a ship to a darkened space station, my boots stomping on the deck so much they echoed.

Brother Rordan abhorred noisy footfalls; all the monks did.

Universe, please stop these flashbacks. I don't need them. I don't want them.

It didn't matter where he'd been, just where he was going.

Or not going. He smiled to himself. He had no intention of leaving the Order.

Dasha stood up on wobbly legs, tears streaming down her face.

She was going to die.

Someone else would come after her father, and he'd die, too.

Then the cyborgs, her friends.

As much as she didn't want to, she had to go to the cockpit and find a way to communicate with someone on Kurkay-2. Swallowing her disgust and shame over what waited for her there, she went back to it.

Dalton still lay on the floor, but he'd rolled over in the *Raider*'s liftoff, and his head was turned away so she couldn't see the gash on his neck. Dasha reached for his covering and dropped it over what she could see of his head and felt a tiny bit better.

"Dasha?"

Cecily's voice crackled through a comm panel. "Oh, my God!" Dasha said. "Can you hear me?"

"Yeah, we're patched in," Cecily said. "Are you all right?"

"Yeah, aside from being an idiot." Relief coursed through her. "How do I land this thing?"

"Well, you don't," said Cecily. "We're going to give you some very specific instructions, okay? And don't freak out."

Dasha's relief immediately evaporated. "What?"

"According to Jason and Lukas, the *Raider* is set to auto-destruct," Cecily said. "In about fourteen minutes. I didn't do it, Dalton did. He had a fucked-up failsafe on his ship, which in retrospect I should've figured out, but it's Janek fucking Dalton, and it's not like he was the sharpest knife in the drawer."

"The ship's going to *explode*?" Dasha shrieked.

"I didn't have time to deactivate it," Cecily said. "And we didn't mean to leave you onboard. But there's a way for you to get out and stay alive."

"It was my fault," Dasha said. "I went exploring and got myself stuck in a stairwell. If I hadn't wandered off…"

"It doesn't matter now," Cecily replied. "There's an escape pod in the deck below you. Get in it, and it'll automatically deploy. You should be coming back to Kurkay-2. It'll take a couple of hours, but a fully operable escape pod will keep you alive for a few days."

"But I won't be in it for a few days, right?"

"No," Cecily said, her voice reassuring. "You'll be coming back here soon. We might have some explaining to do to the transit authorities after they pick up your pod breaking atmosphere, but we'll figure out a plausible lie later. Stay calm and get in the pod, okay?"

Dasha nodded, then remembered that Cecily couldn't see her. "I will, and I'm so sorry."

"Don't worry about it. We'll get you home and deal with everything later."

Fortified at Cecily's promise, Dasha left the cockpit, now noticing that the viewscreen offered a dazzling view of a starscape and the blue and green ball of a planet that was Kurkay-2. She shuffled out of the cockpit, wanting to get in that pod and away from the *Raider* and Dalton's body as soon as possible.

The escape pod's door opened at her touch, she stepped in, and it immediately closed behind her. There was only enough space for her to sit down, with just enough space at her feet for the duffel packed with emergency supplies. "What do I do?" she murmured to herself. How did she launch this thing?

"Self-destruct sequence initiated," a tinny voice said. "Nine minutes to self-destruct. Do you wish to evacuate now?"

The pod was waiting for an answer. "Yeah," said Dasha. "Back to Kurkay-2."

"Kurkay-2 is not the pre-programmed destination."

"Fuck," said Dasha.

"Fuck is not a pre-programmed destination."

"Well, what are they?" Dasha demanded. "I need to get back to Westingtown on Kurkay-2."

"I have a list of pre-selected destinations. The last one added was Glissat, by Captain Janek Dalton at six hundred hours this morning."

The name was unfamiliar to Dasha. "Please tell me it's inhabited."

"Glissat has a population of four hundred and eight as of the last Bravan census. Its residents are devoted to the Great Faith, with its population largely monks belonging to the Order of the Benevolent Stars. At its speed, this escape pod will arrive at the destination in approximately six hours, eight minutes."

"Bloody hell," muttered Dasha. "The Great Faith. I'll never get away from that rock." The religion's most fundamentalist practitioners, including Jason's family in the Zone, didn't support the use of modern technology. Plus, the last thing she wanted to do was spend six hours in an escape pod, hurtling through space.

Well, second to last thing. She wasn't keen on being aboard the *Raider* when it exploded.

Why Glissat? Why would Janek Dalton want to go to a tiny planet no one had ever heard of, full of religious adherents, that would probably be cut off from the rest of the galaxy?

Dasha's breath caught in her throat. There was only one reason she could think of that Dalton would want to go there.

He found Rordan Alexander.

"Okay," she said. "Let's go to Glissat and talk to some monks."

Brother Rordan strolled through the temple's gardens, its flowers and trees all of the night-blooming variety. He'd have a cup of tea after his evening prayers, even though he didn't deserve it when his mind kept wandering to other matters.

And memory fragments kept popping up with increasing regularity.

He paused and closed his eyes, centering himself.

I am in a beautiful garden, surrounded by people who I care about and who care about me. It doesn't matter who I used to be, only who I am now and who I am going forward.

He focused on Glissat's nighttime noises: the chirps and songs of baby Bravan owls, the slight sway of tree branches in the light breeze, the rapid rush of water from the nearby river, and then a loud splash...

Wait, what?

That splash came from something far larger than an animal or monk falling in the river, and Brother Rordan would have helped anyone who took a tumble in it. The larger splash... that was something far more serious.

It was difficult to do so in his slippers, but he still raced to the water, blue robe flapping behind him. He fervently hoped none of the other monks saw him running. Hurrying for anything was antithetical to the Order's mission of peacefulness.

Once on the river bank, he scanned the water in either

direction and saw a man-sized, capsule-shaped device on its side, stuck in some rocks.

"My stars," Brother Rordan said aloud. "What have you brought upon our Order this evening?"

It's a ship.

The only memory of a ship Brother Rordan had was the one that brought him to Glissat, so he knew it wasn't an old one resurfacing.

Pod, his subconscious told him. *It's an escape pod. They're on larger ships in case of emergency.*

Had he ever been in an escape pod?

He didn't dwell on that, not wanting to encourage more memory fragments to come back. Instead, he stood on the river's edge, waves touching his bare ankles and soaking his slippers.

Someone could be in that pod. In fact, it was certain there was someone. If the passenger was alive, they would require help; if dead, the Order would inter them with all the dignity they offered their monks. The only question was getting across the water.

He looked in either direction for something that would keep him and his robe dry and found nothing. He sighed. At least the river was shallow.

He waded through the water until he reached the rocks. This close to the escape pod, he could see a green emergency light inside through a round viewport. A hand slapped at it.

"Thanks be to the stars," Brother Rordan said aloud. "Our visitor is alive."

There was an emergency access panel on the pod's side. He pushed aside its protective flap and pulled the release lever he knew to be there, and the pod's door unsealed with a hydraulic hiss.

Brother Rordan was too shocked at what he'd just done to notice that the door was open. *How did I know to do that?*

But his ruminations were interrupted when a woman's head popped out of the doorway, her tangled dark hair streaked with blond a snarl around her head and eyes bright in the moonlight. "Is this Glissat?" she asked, hauling herself up until she was standing in the pod.

Brother Rordan was too surprised to reply, but he'd forgotten all about the emergency release he happened to know existed.

"Are you an angel?" he asked, taking a couple of steps back.

"I—what?" Her eyes widened.

"There are legends of angels in the stars," Brother Rordan said. "Not all orders believe in them, but I think the Benevolent Stars may change their stance on them now that you're here."

"Oh, no," she said. "I'm not an angel. I'm looking for someone."

"Angels are said to deny their existence in the presence of mortals."

"I'm not," she said. "Really." She stuck out her hand. "I'm Dasha Caron. I'm looking for someone, and it's a long shot, but you might be able to help me."

Brother Rordan still couldn't bring himself to move. He scarcely noticed the cold river water rushing along, soaking his lower body and robe, as he took in the divine sight before him.

Messy hair aside, she was beautiful.

"*Dasha*," he whispered.

Oh, dear.

Dasha withdrew her hand. As she did so, the pod, still on its side, wobbled, and she knew it was only a matter of time before it fell from its rocky perch and into the water. The water didn't seem deep here, but she didn't want to face-plant on a rocky riverbed if she didn't have to. "Could you help me down?" she asked.

The question seemed to snap the man back to attention. "Of course, angel."

"Please don't call me that. Dasha's fine."

"What kind of name is 'Dasha'?"

"One that belonged to my grandmother," she replied. "I didn't catch your name, though."

He helped her out of the pod so she could balance on the largest rock nearby. With an inhuman swiftness, he collected her in his arms and carried her above the water to the shore, comfortably holding her level with his shoulders so she wouldn't get wet. His arms didn't even shake with the strain.

He set her down on the shore. "You didn't tell me your name," Dasha said again.

She could get a better look at him now that they were in a more open area, the light from the twin moons hanging in the sky bright. There was enough light for her to see his eyes clearly, especially now that they were glowing a little.

"Holy shit," she said before she could stop herself. "*Rordan*? Rordan Alexander?"

He froze. "My name is Brother Rordan, my angel."

"Don't start with the 'angel' stuff," Dasha said. "Not that a girl doesn't appreciate a nice nickname once in a while, but this isn't the time. You must be Rordan Alexander."

He shook his head. "If I was ever this person, I'm not now. I'm Brother Rordan, a novice monk with the Order of the Benevolent Stars."

"Your eyes are glowing," Dasha said. "I know you're a cyborg. People are looking for you."

Rordan blinked, and his eyes went back to normal, save for a metallic glint Dasha noticed in the other cyborgs she'd met. "I don't know what a cyborg is," he replied stiffly.

Dasha hated to do this. "Omega-Three-Omega," she said. "You were lured and captured there for a year." She hoped she wasn't to trigger buried memories and unleash latent post-traumatic stress. "You were a soldier with the Zone military. You…"

"I don't remember or acknowledge my past," Rordan said shortly.

"You have a cybernetic kill switch in your head, and people are after you," Dasha blurted. "You have to get away from this place and come with me. It isn't safe here. My escape pod had your coordinates in it, and others might, too."

"I'll take you to the temple," Rordan said as if she hadn't just told him he could be dying. "The fathers will know what to do."

"Are you listening to me?" Dasha said. "People are after you. *Bad* people."

"The stars and universe will always provide," Rordan said, more peacefully than Dasha liked. "Please come with me, my angel. It will be the pleasure of the temple to make sure your stay on the mortal plane is pleasant."

If she went to the temple, she might find someone who could talk sense into Rordan. Unless they were the ones who brainwashed him, but she'd deal with that later.

She dearly hoped she wasn't walking into a trap.

Great Faith monks are peaceful. They take pacifism and respect for all living creatures and all that shit seriously. I probably won't get hurt.

Going with Rordan to the temple was her only option.

She sighed. "Sounds good," she said. "Let's go to that temple."

CHAPTER 3

THE ANGEL, Dasha, kept protesting otherwise as Brother Rordan led her along the path back to the temple. Excitement and disbelief thrummed in his veins, and he couldn't stop thanking the stars and universe for choosing him to bring the angel to the temple's fathers. Surely, they'd know what to do with a divine guest.

He looked down at his robe and suppressed a sigh. It was already drying from his dip in the river, but it was stained and dirt decorated the hem. What a terrible first impression to make to her.

Brother Rordan paused at the door to Father Nelo's private meditation room. His hand hovered, hesitant to knock, unsure if he should interrupt his superior's prayers. It was supremely rude to do so.

He cast a quick glance at the angel. "What?" she said in a loud whisper. "Is there somewhere I can send a transmit here?"

He held a finger to his lips, encouraging her to be quiet.

"Why?" she said, a little louder. She sounded more frustrated, too. "Is there someone in there who can help us out?"

Even though Brother Rordan didn't want to invoke Father Nelo's disappointment in him, he still liked how the angel said "us."

She was on a mission to find you.

In his excitement, he hadn't really dwelled on that fact. Dasha was here for him; she'd known his name and claimed to know details of his old life.

Before he could knock on the door, it opened, revealing a serene-looking Father Nelo. "Brother," the senior monk said in surprise. "Why are you loitering in the hall?"

Before he could form a response, the father saw Dasha, and his eyes widened.

"Hi," she said. "I'm here for Rordan."

"I found her in the river," Brother Rordan said. "I know the Order here doesn't officially believe in such beings, but she's an angel."

To his chagrin, Father Nelo didn't share his wonder. Instead, he coolly regarded Dasha. "Are you?" he asked, more sharply than Brother Rordan liked.

"No," she replied. "And I've been telling him that since he found me. Are you in charge here?"

"I am but one of ten fathers tasked with the well-being of our Order."

"Is that a yes?"

Father Nelo straightened a little. "It is."

"Great," said the angel. "Well, I'm Dasha Caron, and through a combination of stupidity and sheer dumb luck, I ended up on Glissat." She peeked around Father Nelo into his meditation room. "Is there somewhere we can sit down and talk? This will take a while, and I'm sure you have questions."

To Brother Rordan's surprise, Father Nelo gestured for them to step inside. "Of course, Miss Caron. Brother, you as well."

Brother Rordan had never been invited to sit in a father's

private meditation room. Novice monks were never allowed to do so. But his humility at receiving such an honor lessened when he noticed that Dasha didn't carry the same reverence.

Of course, she wouldn't. She was an angel, far elevated above his or Father Nelo's status.

The father gestured to the seat cushions on the floor that surrounded a low table. "Can I get you something to eat or drink?" he asked Dasha. "I'm afraid it isn't the fancier fare you're probably used to, but we do take care to ensure what we have tastes good."

"Maybe in a bit," Dasha said. "And why would you assume I'm used to 'fancier fare'?"

"Your food in the heavens must be better than what we have on the mortal plane," Brother Rordan said.

Father Nelo's answer was less celestial. "You have a distinctive Sidra Prime accent."

That drew a smile from Dasha. The sight of it transformed her face, and he stared for a few seconds until the weight of Father Nelo's words sunk in. "Sidra Prime?" he echoed.

"Yeah," said Dasha. "I moved to Princess Cay twenty-four years ago, when I was four, but I'm originally from the Zone."

"Ah," said Father Nelo, nodding. "I presume Brother Rordan originally hails from the Zone, as well?"

"I think so," said Dasha slowly. "But we're more concerned with where he is now, and we have to find a way off Glissat and back to Kurkay-2, where I live now. Um, is that offer of a drink still on the table?"

"Of course. Do you imbibe, or would you prefer sparkling water? It's derived from a local spring."

"What the hell," said Dasha. "Let's try your *imbibing* drinks." Half a second later, she said, "Sorry, I didn't mean to swear."

Father Nelo was already on his feet. He crossed the

room's short distance to an icebox, where he fetched a large bottle of temple-brewed beer. "No apologies necessary, Miss Caron."

"'Dasha' is fine," she said. "My students called me 'Miss Caron.'"

"Oh, you're a schoolteacher?"

"I was," she said. "Back in Princess Cay. I taught primary school. My life's been upended a little over the last couple of months."

"Guiding children is an important profession," Father Nelo said, returning to the table. He set out two glasses and filled them with beer.

"What about Rordan?" Dasha asked. To Brother Rordan, she said, "You don't drink?"

"Novice monks usually don't partake," Father Nelo replied. "And Brother Rordan never has. Unless you would like a glass this evening?" He turned to Brother Rordan.

"No, thank you." Disappointment pulled at him. He couldn't believe someone as wise and learned as Father Nelo didn't believe an angel was in his midst.

Dasha sipped at her beer, appreciation bringing another small smile to her face. It quickly disappeared, and she said, "Okay. About Rordan and why I'm here."

Father Nelo's head was still bowed in a brief prayer of thanks. "Damn," muttered Dasha. "I should've waited."

The father raised his head and took a sip of his own drink. "Please continue, Dasha."

"How far back should I go?" Dasha said, more to herself than them before she continued. "Well, my father founded a cybernetics company years ago in the Zone. He started it to make inexpensive replacement limbs and organs. You know what the Zone's like. They saw he was doing amazing things, and the military swooped in and developed cyborg technology. It was shut down after a while, but the damage was already done, and too many people had the tech my dad developed in their hands.

"Officially, only one cyborg exists. But a couple of the people who were part of the original cyborg project continued their research illegally, and Rordan here was one of the subjects. Up until around a year ago, he was held against his will on a planet outside the Rims. Omega-Three-Omega."

Brother Rordan had never heard of the place.

"Rordan and a group of other men were rescued, and the survivors are all on Kurkay-2," Dasha continued. "We have strong reason to believe that a private water conglomerate based in the Zone is after the cyborg technology. Rordan is the only unaccounted-for cyborg, and people are after him. One of them dropped by my apartment this morning, and that's part of the reason I'm here now."

"And the person who visited you had a nefarious purpose?" Father Nelo said, then sipped his beer again.

"Yeah, he was a well-known bounty hunter and mercenary we've dealt with before," Dasha said. "He was a terrible person. He was looking for me, my dad, and Rordan. He already knew where Rordan was."

"He *was* a terrible person?" the father asked.

Dasha flushed, and Brother Rordan thought her eyes looked a little glassier than normal. "Yeah. He's, um, dead now."

"I see. Was his death justified?"

Brother Rordan stared at Father Nelo, shocked. "There's no such thing as justifiable death," he said.

"There are exceptions," the father retorted sharply.

What?

"Self-defense," said Dasha. "He attacked me, and he was definitely after Rordan. The coordinates in my escape pod corresponded to Glissat. I think it was keyed to his location somehow, probably through his old military ident chip."

Military ident?

An image of sitting in a bare room full of medical equipment popped into his mind, a man wearing a lab coat injecting something under the skin of his wrist and rattling off a number. "Good luck with your basic training," the man had said. "Try not to get your dick blown off on the frontlines."

Brother Rordan closed his eyes to will away the memory, but instead of fading away, it became stronger. He could smell the antiseptic in the room.

Instinctively, he felt his forearm, just under his elbow, and pressed the skin there. It took a few seconds, but he felt a small, distinct square shape when he prodded it.

He'd known exactly where to look. A chill slithered through him.

"If Janek Dalton—the guy who came after me—knew Rordan's whereabouts, others may, too," Dasha continued. "He was after money, so I doubted he told anyone about Glissat, but it's a possibility. For everyone's safety, he needs to leave with me." She paused. "Unfortunately, I don't have a shuttle or ship available at the moment, so that's why I need to send a transmit back to Kurkay-2 as soon as possible."

"No," said Brother Rordan.

"I beg your pardon?" said Dasha.

Brother Rordan hated to do this when in the presence of a divine being, but she was speaking nonsense. "I can't leave," he said. "This is my home. It has been since I woke up, and the monks here took pity on me and encouraged me to join their ranks." He turned beseeching eyes to Father Nelo. "Please make her understand I mean no disrespect, but I can't go."

But Father Nelo only looked sad. "If what she says is true, it would be best for you to leave Glissat until the threat is passed," he said.

Numbness spread through Brother Rordan at his superior's words, and even though he knew he was supposed to abide by the father's words, he didn't want to. He couldn't. He shook his head, tried to speak, but nothing came out.

"Rordan," said Dasha, voice softer. "Look at me."

She reached out and touched his hand on the tabletop. It was a small gesture, but electrifying all the same. He had to fight the urge to pull away from her in surprise.

"You've been through trauma," she said. "I'm not saying I can fix that, but I can help arrange it so it isn't worse." She looked away for a second. "Um, do you remember anything from before you got here?"

"My mind was blank," Brother Rordan replied. "I remembered my name and how to speak and walk, but that's all. I don't want to remember anything else."

A small sigh escaped Dasha, and she turned to Father Nelo. "Do you know anything about Rordan's background? He was left on Spaceport 44 after Omega-Three-Omega was evacuated."

"Brother Rordan was brought to us via a passenger transport from the Zone," replied Father Nelo. "He had no memory of who he was, nor did he have any money or another place to go. Our temple is a place of healing, and we welcome the poor and indigent. Brother Rordan preferred to stay and pledge as a novice monk."

He didn't remember much of his early days on Glissat. He'd woken up one morning, feeling happy and light as air, pleased to be on this lovely planet with kind people and beautiful foliage.

"For what it's worth, Rordan isn't broke," said Dasha. "Not by a long shot. And your memory loss is probably related to what I told you earlier outside. About your kill switch."

Father Nelo gasped. "Brother, what is she speaking of?"

"Nothing," Brother Rordan replied. "She says I'm part

machine, and there's something in me that could be fatal, but I don't care. I'd rather die happy here than leave."

"It can be fixed," Dasha stressed. "It's already been done. My father performed the surgery on another cyborg." She pinched the bridge of her nose, and he thought he could see the frustration rolling off her in waves. "You're a cyborg. People are after cyborgs. If nothing else, you can come with me, get your kill switch deactivated, and when it's safe, return here and be a monk and make beer for the rest of your life, if you want. But you have to go with me for that to happen."

Brother Rordan crossed his arms over his chest. "No."

"Remember the others," said Father Nelo softly. "If what Dasha says is true, your staying here would put the safety of every monk here in jeopardy. Do you want that on your conscience?"

The father had him there. Something must have shifted in his expression because Dasha's relaxed a little.

"I know the Great Faith adherents prefer not to utilize modern technology that much," said Dasha. "But you must have a way to communicate off-world."

"Of course," Father Nelo said. "Although you should know that the Faith followers in the Brava System are a little more lenient about technology than our counterparts in the Zone. Our temple is climate-controlled, and we use medicine when we're sick." He drained the last of his beer. "Please follow me, and I'll take you to our communication office."

Dasha stood up. Brother Rordan didn't move.

"Rordan?" she asked curiously. "You coming?"

He didn't want to, but the warning look he received from Father Nelo had him on his feet. "Yes."

Father Nelo led Dasha and Rordan through the temple's corridors, walking at a brisk clip. They strode through myriad corridors, the walls decorated with hand-stitched tapestries, until they reached a non-descript, ordinary-looking office. It reminded Dasha of the principal's office at the school she taught at in Princess Cay.

But Rordan was nearly beside himself. He didn't speak, but she saw it in his reaction to the equipment the office housed and Father Nelo's comfort with it. The father gestured to the desk chair. "Please sit down and send your message. Take your time."

"Thank you."

The thintab he gave her was many years out of date, but she could still connect to the galactic net and ping Cecily's transmit address. If Cecily didn't respond, she could try Anders and Valenna next. She mentally ran down the list of addresses she'd memorized until Cecily's face filled the thintab screen.

"Oh, thank God," Cecily said by way of greeting. Her eyes were red-rimmed like she'd been crying. "You're okay, right? You have no idea how fucking panicked we were when the *Raider* took off and you were still onboard, and..." She sniffled. "Oh, my God, Dasha, I'm so sorry. Where are you?"

"Glissat," Dasha said. "And I'm all right. I'll explain in detail what happened when I get back to Westingtown. I don't know how secure this connection is."

"Standard," murmured Father Nelo.

"My friend says it's standard," Dasha repeated.

"In that case, wait to tell me," Cecily said. "You're on Glissat? How the hell did you end up there?"

"Standard connection," Dasha reminded her, bypassing Cecily's question. "We need someone to pick us up."

"Us?"

"I found Rordan," she said triumphantly. She angled the

thintab to show Rordan's face, but he turned away. "He's alive and in one piece."

"I thought the expression was 'alive and well.'"

Dasha's heart sank, and she hated having to deliver bad news. "About that," she said. "He doesn't remember anything."

Cecily tilted her head the side, confused. "What?"

"I'm at a Great Faith temple," Dasha said. "It's all monks. They're very nice." She shot a quick glance at Father Nelo, who beamed at her praise. "They've been very helpful. But Rordan is a novice monk and remembers nothing since he got here."

Cecily's eyebrow lifted. "How the fuck does that happen?" Immediately, she caught herself. "Please tell the monks in the room I didn't mean to say that."

"There's no worry at all," Father Nelo said. "It wasn't directed in anger or spite."

"Rordan doesn't want to leave," Dasha said.

"He has to. He has a thing in his head that could kill him."

"And his memory loss is probably related to that," Dasha said. "I agree with you, and so does his superior monk." She turned to Father Nelo. "Did I get that right?" She didn't want to be disrespectful in the wake of the senior monk's kindness.

"Yes."

"Okay," said Cecily. "I can't get over there on the *Gray Ghost* since your dad's basically turned her into a hospital until Serena has her baby. The smallest and lightest ship I can think of right now is Adam and Esme's *Dragonfly*. They'll probably let me borrow her so I can pick you up. I'll be there in a few hours."

"Please be careful," said Dasha. "Is the *Dragonfly* armed? Janek Dalton knew where Rordan is, and that means others probably do, too. You could run into trouble."

"Ah, shit." She screwed up her face. "Sorry, I didn't mean

to say that. I think the *Dragonfly* has basic weaponry, but I doubt anyone's going to think a ship her size is a threat. Traveling incognito is the way to go right now."

"Are you sure?"

"Yeah." Cecily scrubbed her face with her hands. "I can't tell you how glad I am that you're okay, Dasha. And Rordan, too. Can you send me your coordinates? Is there a landing site nearby?"

"Yes," said Father Nelo. "We have a landing pad for delivery ships." He placed his hand on Dasha's shoulder. "May I?"

Dasha vacated the seat, and the monk took her place, where he rattled off the temple coordinates to Cecily. "May the stars and universe guide and be with you," he said, inclining his head.

Cecily looked a little confused but did likewise.

"Be safe," Dasha said. "I'll see you in a few hours."

CHAPTER 4

"NO."

Brother Rordan hated the look on Dasha's face, a combination of disappointment and frustration, but that didn't change his mind. He crossed his arms over his chest and glared at her the best he could.

He wasn't one to disobey Father Nelo, either, but the last thing he wanted was to get aboard the olive-drab, banged-up *Dragonfly*. Her hull was pitted and scarred, like she'd been in a fight and lost. It didn't look safe. He thought about how he found Dasha in the river and wondered what kind of technology she had to rely on.

But it wasn't just the *Dragonfly* that had him anxious. There was something about her pilot that made him uneasy. Cecily Barris looked innocuous enough, even sweet with her big brown eyes and dark curls, but there was something else about her that he couldn't put his finger on. Something simmered under her innocent-looking exterior that made his skin crawl.

"There's a climate-controlled coffin in the hold. Put your friend's body in there with the others, and I'll deal with them later."

Those words, spoken by her, rang through his head as clearly as the monks' dinner bell, despite her not saying anything beyond introducing herself.

Aaron Bell.

The name of the man she'd been referring to was Aaron Bell. Brother Rordan watched him collapse to the deck on Cecily Barris's ship.

I remember that.

Other images tried to break through, but he fought them back and resisted the urge to clap his hands over his eyes like a little kid to fend them off. He knew the gesture would be useless, but the temptation to do it remained.

"Please get on the ship," Dasha murmured. "I know you two didn't get off on the right foot, at least that's what I'm guessing, but she's here to help. She saved you before."

He turned to Father Nelo, who waited beside Cecily. To his surprise and shame, the father's expression was one of disappointment and tightly controlled anger.

"You will go with them for your surgery," said Father Nelo. "When it is safe to do so, you may return and resume your studies. But your continued presence here poses a risk to the rest of us until this settles over."

"And it will," said Cecily quickly.

"Go on," said Dasha, nudging him. "If it helps you any, I'll be there, right beside you."

It would help, but he still didn't trust Cecily.

He closed his eyes again and prayed, hoping the stars were listening and would tell him what to do. But when he opened them, the first thing he saw was Father Nelo's disapproving look, and he had his answer.

He was going to Kurkay-2, and he would undergo surgery to fix the thing Dasha and Cecily said he had in his head. Then he would come back home to the temple where there wasn't anything to remind him of his old life and pick up where he left off in his studies.

———

Brother Rordan was quiet during the trip, refusing all offers of food and drink from Dasha. "How are you not hungry?" she asked. "I've missed dinner, and I'm starving. Who knew crash-landing an escape pod on a religious compound could do that?"

"I'm fine." He wasn't. His stomach rumbled, and he hoped she didn't notice. But he couldn't bring himself to eat just yet.

"Suit yourself." Dasha left the room she'd brought him to after the *Dragonfly* broke Glissat's atmosphere, a lounge area that looked like it was a child's space at one point. Toys were stacked in a crate next to the beaten-up, deck-locked couch that was probably older than the ship. The letter "R" was written on a wall over and over, the marks only half-scrubbed away.

Brother Rordan waited, hands on his lap, until Dasha returned with a tray of ready meals, already reheated, and cups of tea. "It's nothing fancy," she said, "but it'll fill you up."

The smell was nearly overpowering, but he didn't want to give in just yet. "No, thank you."

"Quit being a martyr and have something to eat," she said, picking up a tray and fork. "Would it be terrible of me if I said 'the angel commands it'?"

"Yes."

"Okay, then I won't. But I heard your stomach growling. Cecily probably heard it in the cockpit."

"I don't like Cecily."

Dasha's eyes widened, and her hand hovered between the

tray and her mouth. The bit of food she'd speared dropped off the fork, but she didn't notice. "Why not?"

"I don't trust her."

Understanding dawned over Dasha's face. "Oh, right. Your subconscious probably remembers her, or something. Look, she's a little rough around the edges and kind of terrifying when you first meet her, I get that. But she's good people." She paused and picked up her fallen food. "Yeah, she's good people."

Brother Rordan wasn't sure he liked how Dasha had to repeat that as if she had to reassure herself of what Cecily was.

He was loath to talk about his memories resurfacing. But even though Dasha was the one to urge him to board the *Dragonfly* and upend his life and she likely wasn't an angel, there was something about her that made her approachable. Warm.

Dasha pointed her fork at the tray. "If nothing else, just have some tea. Do it for me."

She wasn't going to let up on that, was she?

"It isn't drugged," she added.

If Brother Rordan hadn't worried about being drugged before, he did now. When his eyes met Dasha's, he could tell she'd just realized her misstep almost as soon as the words were out of her mouth.

"Ah, nuts," she muttered. "Look, if it'll make you feel better, I can sample your food before you eat something. And you should." With that, she speared a bite of his ready meal and popped it in her mouth, followed by a quick gulp of his tea. "I hope you aren't squeamish about germs."

"Not at all. They were created by the stars and universe," he replied.

Dasha was quiet as she took a bite from her own meal and considered his words. "Do you believe that if something was created by the universe, it has to be good?"

Some of the tension that he hadn't realized he'd been holding between his shoulders dissipated. This was a subject he felt a little more comfortable with, even though he was still a novice monk. "Everything starts off good," he said. "It's one of the basic tenets of the Great Faith. We're *born* good. Our external environments, our choices, all of that determines whether one stays that way. Anyone sentient is fallible."

"I was thinking more along the lines of an ion storm," Dasha said. "Or an earthquake."

Brother Rordan had contemplated the reasons for such terrible events when he first arrived on Glissat, and after months of study still couldn't offer an acceptable answer to that kind of question. Even the fathers disagreed on such matters, and he'd never considered it his place to insert himself into such a debate with minds better educated than his.

And now Dasha, the angel, was asking his opinion about natural disasters like his thoughts were important.

"There's considerable controversy about these matters," he said.

"Yeah, that doesn't surprise me. What do you think about that, in the context of your faith?"

He'd just been presented with an opportunity to shed some light on the Great Faith to someone who, despite her insistence on going with her aboard the *Dragonfly*, and had been nothing but polite and respectful to him since they met. Someone who he could have introduced to the Great Faith.

Someone who could have taken advantage of him, manipulated him into doing what she wanted when he thought she was an angel fallen out of the sky.

"I don't know," he said. "Those phenomena on their own aren't inherently bad or evil, but they're usually only spoken of in the context of potential harm to sentient populations. That's why we hear about them and why we fear them."

Dasha didn't immediately reply, and he couldn't read her expression. He fought the urge to fidget in his seat like a kid.

Finally, she said, "I don't think you learned to speak like that in the military."

The comment caught him off-guard. "I beg your pardon?"

"You're clearly educated," she said. "Well beyond the minimum requirements in the Zone. I bet you have at least an undergraduate degree. I wonder why someone with that would choose to go to the Brava border to fight and then be recruited into a cyborg experiment."

Before he could think better of it, Brother Rordan blurted, "Education and intelligence aren't synonymous."

"Well yeah, no shit." She made a face. "Sorry. I didn't mean to say that."

"No apologies necessary. Although, I don't want to further speculate on any secular education I may have had."

"Okay. I can respect that."

"Thank you."

Dasha changed the subject. "Do you want to know about who we're meeting on Kurkay-2, at least? Bring you up to speed?"

"I don't want to talk about cyborgs and kill switches right now." He didn't know if he would ever want to. All he wanted was to get the stars-damned thing out of his head and return to Glissat, where he belonged.

"All right," said Dasha. "Do you like kids? Adam and Esme—the couple who own this ship—have a little girl, four years old. And our friend Serena's pregnant. She's the only female cyborg out there."

"I don't have any experience with children."

Maybe he had, in his forgotten life, but he thought if he did, the mention of the kids in Dasha's cyborg circle would tug on phantom heartstrings. But there was nothing, besides the knowledge that as a monk, he would never have children.

"I do," said Dasha. "I like kids and I want my own someday. I miss teaching."

Brother Rordan recalled her saying she taught.

"Why not teach on Kurkay-2?" he asked.

"We're living in and around the Westingtown settlement, and it doesn't have enough children to establish a school. It's a very new community, and it's mostly adults there, with a few little kids. I'm going back to Sidra Prime as soon as I can anyway," she explained. "Once it's safe to do so."

"After my surgery is performed." He'd never see her again, and for some reason, the notion made him sad.

A notion that was irrational and insane. He'd met her a few hours ago.

"About that." Dasha set aside her tea. "Even after your kill switch is fixed, there's still the matter of the rest of the tech in your body and the people who after that tech. We both heard Father Nelo back at the temple. You can't go back until that Zone water dealer is out of the picture."

Brother Rordan wanted to argue with her over that, but the logical part of his brain told him Dasha was right.

She hesitated, carefully parsing her words. "Haven't you noticed your cybernetic functions?" she asked. "Or anyone else? Exceptional strength, night vision, data readouts in your eyes, ports in your body?"

Another memory shard stabbed at him. "Ports," he murmured to himself.

"What?"

But Dasha's voice sounded far away as another memory shard stabbed at him.

"Cover them up," Rordan said. He was lying on his back on a hard table, examining his left arm. The room's harsh yellow lights making his ports look like the tumors they were, irregular and dark and ugly against his skin.

"All I have here is syntho-skin. The really old shit that isn't

on the market anymore." A face peered over him, blocking out some of the yellow light. "One good scratch and it'll peel right off. It's not worth it. Just fucking wear long sleeves."

"I'm paying you to make me normal again."

"I don't know what you are, but 'normal' isn't it. I told you—"

"Do it!"

It was the longest flashback Brother Rordan had had so far, and if he wasn't already sitting, his knees would have buckled beneath him.

Who was that?

What did he mean by "old syntho-skin"?

Brother Rordan reached for his left wrist, and his fingers traced lightly dimpled skin on his inner wrist. The texture was off, not matching the surrounding skin.

He'd noticed that before, when he arrived on Glissat, but never thought much of it. He hadn't wanted to know.

Brother Rordan picked at one of the odd-textured patches on his arm. The skin crinkled under his touch.

"What are you doing?" asked Dasha in horrified awe.

He didn't answer. Instead, he peeled back the skin, revealing a port like the ones in the temple's office comp.

It didn't hurt, and there was only a little blood where it was pulled off. The small piece of whatever he'd just ripped off his body didn't feel like real skin. It was too thick, for one thing, and it was already starting to crumble in his fingers, like a piece of stale bread.

What am I?

For a second, he was terrified more memories would return and suffocate him if they were anything like the one that just resurfaced. But nothing came flooding back; his only emotion was cold fear.

Stars and universe, what do I do now? I need your guidance!

"Where's the bathroom?" he asked hoarsely.

"There's one in the captain's quarters. Rordan, what happened?"

He couldn't bring himself to speak, only to bolt from the lounge.

The last thing he wanted was for the angel who fell from the stars to see proof of him being the monster he always feared he was.

CHAPTER 5

DASHA WAS at a loss for how to help Rordan.

She could have smacked herself for reacting the way she did when he pulled off what looked like a chunk of poorly applied syntho-skin from his arm. *Stupid, stupid, stupid.*

He'd obviously been having some kind of flashback right before that happened, and she'd made things worse. He'd had enough upheaval in recent years to last several lifetimes; the least she could've done was try to be supportive when he ripped syntho-skin off his body and revealed a forgotten wrist port.

I should've been gentler with the questions. I shouldn't have asked him about remembering old cyborg reflexes. If he was here, my dad would have yelled at me for that.

He would know how to help Rordan, beyond the need to deactivate his kill switch.

But wouldn't Rordan have noticed an ocular data readout? Jason Formosa, Lukas Best, and Anders Barris all reported having that feature: an ever-present stream of information scrolling along their lower vision, revealing information about external stimuli. Lukas's was the most sophisticated, probably because he'd had a whole team behind his cybernetic transformation while the other cyborgs were operated on by a single doctor.

But Serena didn't have a data readout. It was possible that Rordan didn't have one, either. Whoever had done his piss-poor syntho-skin grafts obviously wasn't a qualified practitioner, which would account for his amnesia.

That meant at least one more person knew about cyborgs and Omega-Three-Omega.

She sighed and massaged her temples, feeling a tension headache coming on. This kept getting worse and worse.

What the hell happened at Spaceport 44 after Cecily left him there?

Cecily had delved into the spaceport's history before and came up with very little information about it. It was owned by a numbered corporation, like so many other tiny civilian spacebound hubs. It had an open docking policy and an abundance of cheap, borderline-illegal shuttle fuels available for sale. The scant amount of data available on the galactic net painted it as a place with no permanent inhabitants, the few storefronts constantly rotating tenants, rife with crime, and a hotbed of darfin dealing. It was a good place to go if one felt like being robbed or worse.

Dasha froze.

What if Rordan went to Spaceport 44 as a way to commit suicide?

A chill coursed through her at the notion, followed by compassion and pain, mingling together. Her heart ached for him.

Would checking up on him right now be considered a boundary violation? Or would he understand her concern for him was placed out of friendship?

Bracing herself, she left the galley, then made her way through the *Dragonfly* to the captain's cabin.

The door was open, the cabin's main lights off. The only

light came from the thin illumination strips inset on the walls above the deck. "Rordan?" she said, then quickly corrected herself. "Brother Rordan?"

The bathroom door was closed, a thin beam of light leaking at the bottom across the threadbare carpet bolted to the bedroom deck. It opened when she called him, and Rordan stepped out. "Yes?"

"Are you all right?" She knew it was a stupid question, but she still needed to ask it.

"I don't know." He held up his hands, and in the light offered from the bathroom, she could see that he'd pulled off chunks of syntho-skin to reveal ports in his wrists and arms.

It wasn't the only thing Dasha noticed. His hands shook, fine tremors coursing through them.

"I'm sure there's more," he said, voice hoarse. "I checked all over, but I didn't find any more patches. But it isn't just this thing that's in my head, is it?"

"No."

"What else is it?"

"None of the cyborgs I know are the same," said Dasha. "The other ones from Omega-Three-Omega all have different enhancements. From what they've told me, you weren't there that long, about a year."

"How long were the others there?"

"Up to four years," she replied. "I only recently met them, so I don't know all of their stories." She knew not to push.

He quieted again and sat down on the bed. The mattress was bare, stripped of linens that were now in use at Adam and Esme's apartment in Westingtown. Dasha hesitated, unsure if her presence was still wanted.

He surprised her and patted the space next to him. "Sit."

She did so. "You talked about vision," Brother Rordan said.

"Yeah."

"My eyes glowed in the bathroom. They've never done that before. All I had to do was think about the possibility of having night vision, and then it happened." As if to illustrate his point, he turned brightly glowing eyes to her. "It's like every light in this cabin is turned on."

Rordan's night vision didn't bother her, but his scrutiny made her feel a little self-conscious. His eyes studied her face as if memorizing her features. Maybe he was.

For some reason, she liked that.

"Your eyes have little silver flecks in them," he said.

She blinked. "They're brown."

"With silver," he said. "Almost like stars." He paused, and a frown marred his face. "That sounds exceptionally trite, doesn't it? I must have heard that before somewhere."

"Maybe you said it to a partner."

He shook his head. "No. About your eyes looking like stars. It's something out of a bad poem." His mouth quirked in a small smile.

If he could see the color the compliment brought to her cheeks, he didn't show it. "Trite or not, thank you."

"Can you help me with something?"

She tilted her head, surprised by the question. "Sure."

"You said your escape pod located me with the military ident chip I'm supposed to have in me," he said. "I think I know where it is. I have to remove it as soon as possible." A harsh, humorless laugh escaped him. "I should have considered that before we left the temple."

Oh, no.

It wasn't for nothing that Dasha chose to become a teacher instead of following in her father's footsteps. Even seeing a little bit of blood when one of her students scraped a knee had knots forming in her stomach. Seeing the thin, precise line of blood when a laser scalpel did its work? She would've passed out on an operating room floor if she was foolish enough to pursue nursing or medicine.

She swallowed, wanting to refuse but knowing she couldn't. He was right. She couldn't believe she hadn't thought about removing his chip before they left Glissat.

"If you'd left your chip there, the temple still could have been in danger," she said. "At least we're a little better defended on Kurkay-2."

And the emphasis was on "little." The law enforcement was sparse; the residents of the tiny Westingtown community and surrounding farms tended to keep to themselves, and their weapons tended to be the kind that could take down an animal for dinner, not a militia. Dasha dearly hoped that her neighbors and acquaintances weren't going to be massacred thanks to Wilton Intergalactic Fluid Technology.

"You may have the necessary technology to destroy it," Rordan pointed out. "But you haven't answered my question. Can you help me remove it?"

Dasha closed her eyes, wishing she carried the religious faith Rordan did. It would come in handy right about now.

I hate the sight of blood. I hate it so, so much.

But Rordan was counting on her. In a way, everyone else in Westingtown was, too.

"Yeah," she said, her voice sounding stronger than she felt. "Of course. Let's see what we have available onboard to do some amateur surgery."

Now that Brother Rordan could acknowledge how his body had changed, he noticed more things about Dasha.

It wasn't just her eyes, although they were beautiful. So was the rest of her, which he felt guilty for noticing, but he brushed that aside as best he could. Her shoulder-length, sun-bleached brown hair shone, and he found himself longing to touch it and see if it was as soft as it looked. She was shorter than him, the top of her head only reaching his shoulders.

It wasn't just her appearance that made her special. No, there was something else: kindness and patience.

Dasha puttered around the *Dragonfly*'s living quarters, finally locating a small laser scalpel and skin sealant in a medical kit in the lounge. They holed up in the bathroom, where the lighting was sufficient, and they could easily clean up any bloody mess that might ensue. Her hands shook, and he suspected she was more nervous than she was willing to let on.

"You don't have to do this," he said gently.

She shook her head. "No, I'm fine. I want to help you with this. Do you know where your military ident chip is?"

He lifted his robe's oversized sleeve and tapped the inside of his left arm, about ten centimeters below his elbow crease. He could feel the distinct impression of a square chip embedded in his arm, and its scar was faint but still discernible. "There are two," he said. "I think this is the military ident chip."

Dasha nodded. "Makes sense. The Zone chips are inserted above the right wrist, and they're really tiny." She shifted uncomfortably from foot to foot. "Um, I couldn't find a topical anesthetic."

"I'm sure I'll be fine." If nothing else, the pain would give him something tangible to focus on.

"Okay. And you should know I've never done this before."

"Neither have I."

She gave him a weak smile. "I'll try my best not to tear you up too much."

Dasha activated the laser scalpel, making a tiny incision along the original scar. A hiss of pain escaped Brother Rordan, and when he saw her face pale, he forced himself into silence.

The last thing either of them needed was her fumbling with the laser scalpel and nicking something vital.

In that second, he prayed to the stars and universe that they would see fit *not* to send another traumatic flashback his way.

She stepped back after a few seconds, staring at the wound in his arm. "I forgot to look for sterile glove solution," she said, voice shaking as much as her hands had.

Brother Rordan looked down. The gash was longer than he expected it would be, and he surprised himself when he felt a wave of nausea crest over him at the sight of his own blood. But he calmly patted the wound until his fingers pinched the subcutaneous military ident chip, then plucked it from his skin. He dropped it on the bathroom's sink, pain and blood temporarily forgotten as he stared at it. Beneath the blood, it was gold and silver striped, almost resembling a piece of jewelry.

Dasha looked at it, then back to his arm. The laser scalpel dropped to the deck, her eyes rolled back in her head, and her knees crumpled beneath her.

"Oh, stars above," muttered Brother Rordan, neatly catching her before she fell to the floor.

My reflexes were inhumanly fast.

He shook away that revelation out of concern for Dasha. He hauled her to the adjoining bedroom and tried to get her to sit up with limited success on the bed. "Sorry," she mumbled.

"Was it the blood?"

"The blood and the bloody chip." She shuddered. "Do you need help with sealing the giant slash I put in you?"

"Not at all. Just sit tight."

He returned to the bathroom, noting that blood now stained his robe, and sighed. It would be difficult to remove the stains by hand, the monks' preferred method of laundering.

But when he pushed back the sleeve, he found the wound was already healing, his skin rapidly knitting itself back together before his eyes. Within a minute, his skin was back to normal.

Stars and universe.

Dasha found Cecily in the cockpit, leaning back in the pilot's seat as lazily as one might in a café. But her pose was deceptively casual; she was a lethal force to be reckoned with.

"Hey, do you have a minute?" Dasha asked. She felt like an idiot for what she was about to have to admit to her.

"Yeah." Cecily pressed something on the control panel and whirled around in her seat to face Dasha. "What's up?"

"We removed Rordan's military ident," Dasha began, but she was interrupted when Cecily shot to her feet.

"Oh, *fuck*!" Cecily yelped, and nearly knocked over Dasha in her haste for the cockpit's doorway. "Fuck! Is he dying?"

"What? No." Dasha grabbed Cecily's arm. "He's fine. The wound's already healing on its own, it's actually pretty freaky." Rordan showed her his arm after she'd come to, marveling at the way the flesh healed itself. "He panicked and flushed the chip down the toilet, is all."

Cecily stared at her, aghast. "What?"

"He was worried about attracting unfriendlies back to Kurkay-2 and found it in his arm. I, uh, don't do so well with blood and had to sit down after we did some impromptu surgery in the bathroom. There isn't any blood where there shouldn't be," she quickly added.

"You didn't know that military ident chips are keyed to kill switches?"

The thought hadn't occurred to Dasha, and cold fear slammed into her at the risk they'd just taken. "They are?"

"Didn't your father tell you? Or even me or Jason?"

"Not that I recall, but I tend to tune out around medical talk." Dasha's knees went weak, and for a second, she thought she might faint again.

Cecily barreled past Dasha, stalking through the ship's corridors until she reached the captain's cabin. Dasha could have cried with relief when she saw Rordan milling outside the lounge, alive and upright. His expression darkened when he saw Cecily. "Is everything okay?" he asked.

"You're still alive," Cecily said flatly.

"Of course, by the grace of the stars."

"Good," she said. "You could have accidentally killed yourself. Frankly, I'm not sure why you're still standing. I saw your blueprints."

"I beg your pardon?" Rordan asked.

"The data that Garrett Jacoby kept when he enhanced you," Dasha said. "The chip you just ripped out of your arm is supposed to be connected to the kill switch in your head. Remove the chip, trigger the switch. Get it?"

"Yes."

Before Cecily could admonish him further, Rordan held out his arm. There wasn't so much as a trace of a scar. "Completely healed," he announced, beaming. "By the grace of the stars and universe."

Cecily stared at Rordan, her expression inscrutable, then at Dasha. After a moment of tense silence, she said, "You flushed the chip down the toilet?"

Dasha nodded.

"I'll have the waste compactor ejected," she said. "The ship will get a fine for illegal dumping, so we'll have to reimburse Adam and Esme for the expense. And by 'we,' Dasha, I mean you." Before she turned back toward the cockpit, she added,

"Don't do any more medical procedures onboard. Captain's orders."

It was late morning when the *Dragonfly* broke Kurkay-2's atmosphere, and Brother Rordan felt surprisingly alert for someone who had been awake so long.

But he was always like that, wasn't he? The other monks at the temple noticed it, too: Brother Rordan rarely needed more than three or four hours of sleep and could skate by on even less, if necessary. It was a feature he was proud of.

And a feature, he knew now, that was undoubtedly the result of his cybernetic enhancements.

Dasha didn't seem to be holding up as well, he noted when they strapped themselves into jumpseats just before the ship started her descent. There was a lethargy to her motions that betrayed her exhaustion, and her eyes were shadowed with dark half-moons.

But she still gave him a smile and squeezed his hand when the ship's heavy air engines engaged. Brother Rordan's heart gave a funny little flip in his chest at the sight and feel of her.

He could blame that on his cyborg heart, but he knew it was caused by Dasha. As a novice monk, he shouldn't be experiencing it, but for now, he'd let himself enjoy it.

He picked up the noises the ship made while it prepared for landing, and he could faintly pick up Cecily's voice from the cockpit as she spoke with the planet's transit authorities. He tuned out most of it, instead focusing on Dasha, who now looked like she was ready to fall asleep despite the noise. As it was, he nudged her shoulder when the *Dragonfly* finally stilled, her engines shut off, and she jerked her head, fully awake.

"Sorry," she said and yawned. "I can't believe I dozed off

like that." She fumbled with her jumpseat's safety straps and stood up, her balance wavering.

Brother Rordan automatically reached a hand to steady her. She accepted it, then just as quickly let go. He tried not to feel bereft at the loss of contact.

"My dad is going to want to speak to you," she said. "And me, too, since I had that trip from hell in that escape pod." She rubbed her eyes. "You'll have to tell him everything, including the chip." A yawn escaped her. "I'm glad we told Cecily, even though she was pissed."

As much as Brother Rordan distrusted Cecily, he had to admit that she'd helped him when she ensured his ident chip's destruction.

Why didn't the old me think to have it removed when my ports were grafted over?

He shook his head as if he could clear away those thoughts. *Don't think about that.*

He didn't want to encourage more memories to return. The person he used to be must have wanted them erased for a reason; he knew he wouldn't be able to reconcile the old and new Rordans.

He *liked* the new Brother Rordan.

They took a trip via flitter through a small, but modern-looking settlement Dasha and Cecily told him was called Westingtown, where both of them lived in apartments: Cecily with her partner, who Brother Rordan had apparently known in his old life, and Dasha alone.

I shouldn't be pleased that Dasha's alone. I shouldn't even care about it, or that her eyes are so pretty…

The flitter tilted to the side a little, and Cecily uttered a barely concealed curse as she quickly righted it. "Sorry," she said. "We'll be at the *Gray Ghost* soon."

Brother Rordan's breath hitched. The name was familiar.

A body hitting the floor…

A chill slithered down his spine, and the thought that he was the next to die echoed in his mind. He felt sick.

Dasha noticed it and slid across the back passenger seat to be a little closer to him. "Hey," she said quietly. "Are you okay? You look a little green around the gills."

"I beg your pardon?" His voice was strained.

"Do you get motion sick? It would be weird if you were affected by a flitter and not an old ship like the *Dragonfly*, but stranger things have happened."

He gave her a tight smile. "No, it's not that."

"Want to talk about it?"

He did, desperately. But not with Cecily so close to them.

"Not yet," he said and hoped that answer would suffice for now.

CHAPTER 6

"NO."

Dasha felt like crying. She'd dealt with plenty of obstinate people before—small children weren't exactly known for keeping a handle on their emotions—but so rarely with an adult, particularly one who needed help.

Her gaze followed Rordan's, up the ramp that led to the *Gray Ghost*. Her father had already descended it and shaken Rordan's hand by way of greeting, then offered the same apology he'd given to every cyborg he'd met so far.

But Rordan refused to board the *Ghost*. And Dasha had a pretty good idea as to why, but she desperately hoped he could put aside his fear and let Dr. Caron conduct a checkup, if not his surgery.

"Brother Rordan," she said, deliberately using his title. "The sooner you get looked at, the sooner you can go back to Glissat."

"You made it clear that I can't go back to Glissat until whatever company is after me will leave me alone."

"This is one step in that direction," Dasha said. A wheedling note had crept into her voice, but she didn't care. "*Please.*"

Rordan turned to face her and lowered his voice. "I've been on that ship before."

"Yeah, it's the one that brought you to that spaceport."

"People died there," he said.

A few of the tears that Dasha managed to hold at bay escaped. "I know," she said. "But the diagnostic equipment my dad needs to use is on that ship. The closest hospital is over two hundred kilometers away, and it wouldn't have appropriate staff or facilities to help you."

A muscle in Rordan's jaw clenched, but he didn't reply.

"I'll go with you," she said. "You don't have to do the surgery today. Dad will check you out, make sure you're not about to die, and then you can think about your options, okay?"

She waited an agonizing moment while he stared at the ramp, at her father, and back to her. Finally, he bit out, "Fine."

Dasha exhaled a sigh of relief. "Oh, thank God."

His robe billowed out behind him as he stalked up the ramp, Dasha behind him. "Keep it quick," she muttered to her father. "I doubt he'll want to be operated on today."

Dr. Caron nodded. "Noted. Mr. Alexander, Dasha, please follow me."

Rordan froze for a second, and Dasha nearly crashed into him. "Oh," he said. "That's supposed to be my last name."

Dr. Caron was unfazed. "Do you have a preference for something else?"

"I'm a novice monk at the Glissat temple, so 'Brother Rordan' is sufficient."

"Of course. Follow me, Brother."

The *Gray Ghost*'s interior was so over the top in decor that it bordered on tacky. The metallic-flocked paper covering the corridors' walls nearly glowed under the lights, and the deck was carpeted. The cockpit, Dasha knew, had velvet-covered seats. All in all, it was sort of awful, but Cecily explained she acquired the ship as is and never saw fit to change it.

But judging by the tense set of Rordan's shoulders, she guessed he wasn't silently judging the ship's decorating scheme.

A very pregnant Serena Glazer met them outside the *Ghost*'s sickbay door and smiled when she saw Dasha. "Hi!" she said and held out her arms to hug her.

Dasha liked Serena; everyone did. Her pregnancy, entering its ninth month, had been very unexpected given her cyborg status, and difficult thus far. "How are you feeling?"

Serena rested a hand on her stomach. "Better than the last time I saw you, but I'm looking forward to meeting my mini-me and not being pregnant anymore."

"What, you and Matthias aren't thinking about giving this one a sibling?"

"I know you're joking, but if you'd said that to me a week ago, I might've smacked you. I don't think I ever want to do this again. We're just really relieved that it looks like we're all right." She turned to Dr. Caron and Rordan. "I'm so sorry, I've forgotten my manners." She stuck out her hand. "Serena Glazer. You must be Rordan Alexander."

Rordan shook her proffered hand. "Yes."

"I'm a cyborg, too," she said. "A more advanced model, with a feature I didn't know about." She patted her belly, but there was affection in the gesture.

Rordan looked horrified. "Were you subjected to a breeding program?"

"What? No," she said. "My partner, Matthias, is the father. I didn't know I could get pregnant since my whole body was enhanced. In retrospect, I should've given that some consideration. But we're excited to be parents," she added. "We don't know if we're having a boy or a girl yet. We want it to be a surprise."

"Serena," said Dr. Caron gently.

"Right." She stepped out of the way. "Sorry for holding you up. I'm going to the lounge for a snack anyway. Dasha, want to come with me?"

"I'm going in with Rordan," she said. "Some other time?"

"Of course. I'll see you in a bit."

Serena left them, and they walked into the sickbay.

Dr. Caron directed Rordan to the sickbay's single diag bed, and after a second's hesitation, he sat on it. Dasha gave him what she hoped was a reassuring smile.

"I received a message from Cecily while you were en route back to Kurkay-2," Dr. Caron said. "She didn't want to say too much since she didn't trust the *Dragonfly*'s encryption, but I gather you've lost your memory."

Rordan nodded. Dasha could see his shoulders tense through his billowy monk's robe. "That's what I'm told."

"Yet, you knew your name?" Dr. Caron tapped at the screens of a few instruments. Dasha knew he'd had to modify some of them to work on cyborgs, and for Serena's maternal care, but she didn't know the extent of the changes.

"The first thing I remember is waking up in the infirmary of the Order of the Benevolent Stars," said Rordan. "The monks said I was dropped off there by a commercial passenger transport working out of the Zone. Glissat is open to pilgrims, and I later learned that they accept indigent people into their temple, as well. The monks were very welcoming, and I felt it was divine intervention that led me there.

"I don't know if I was a Great Faith adherent before I ended up there," he continued. "But Glissat and the monks there made me into a believer. And the stars, of course," he quickly added, looking up at the ceiling as if they were expecting gratitude.

Ordinarily, Dasha would've ignored the gesture. But since she'd ended up surviving being blasted into open space in an escape pod and crash-landing on the same settlement that welcomed Rordan with open arms, she found herself questioning her lack of spiritual faith.

The pod's coordinates were matched to Rordan's location via his old military ident chip. That wasn't divine intervention.

But thinking of being launched into space from the *Raider* made her think of Janek Dalton and how she'd killed him. She'd managed to put that out of her mind until now.

God damn it.

She would have to go back to her apartment, the scene of the crime, sooner rather than later.

She forced all thoughts of Dalton out of her mind and focused on Rordan as he answered her father's questions. Rordan had had occasional flashbacks since his arrival on Glissat, mostly of a place he described as a lab that could be on the mysterious Spaceport 44 or the one on Omega-Three-Omega. He'd also had a couple that were probably related to the *Gray Ghost*.

"I don't want any more memories to return," Rordan said.

"Aren't you interested in knowing your past?" Dr. Caron asked gently.

Rordan's response was immediate. "No."

"You may have family or friends who are looking for you."

"I doubt that," Rordan said. "I think the logical assumption is that my lack of ties made me an ideal candidate for cybernetic experiments."

He was right. From what Dasha knew, all of the cyborgs had scant social circles. The possible exception was Anders Barris, although he'd thought Cecily was dead for years before they reconnected.

"I'm not interested in being the person I used to be," Rordan continued. "I don't know what caused my amnesia, but I don't want it corrected. I want to ensure the safety of the temple, and then return there when I can." As if to illustrate his point, he defiantly crossed his arms over his chest.

Dr. Caron nodded, but Dasha could tell he was disappointed. "In that case, I'm going to conduct a physical exam and assess your fitness for the surgery. Do you have somewhere to stay? I'm sure Cecily won't mind your staying aboard the *Ghost*."

"Absolutely not. As soon as I can, I want to leave this ship."

"He can stay with me," Dasha blurted.

It would be an ideal situation: he didn't want to stay on the *Gray Ghost*. Dasha didn't want to return to the apartment, alone, where she killed someone. She wasn't entirely sure that the ghost of Janek Dalton wouldn't haunt her, and if he didn't, her own memories would keep her on edge.

Dr. Caron tilted his head to the side, giving Dasha a look she recalled all too well. She saw it a lot when she was a teenager in Princess Cay, trying to convince her father to let her go to a party hosted by older university students.

But she wasn't a teenager anymore. "It'll be fine," she said. "I have enough space for the two of us, and we get along okay, right?" She gave him what she hoped was a convincing smile.

Something lit up in Rordan's eyes, and he gave her one back. *Oh, God.* The last time she'd seen that look, he was convinced she was an angel.

He needed to do it more.

"Yes," he said. "I'll stay with Dasha."

The flitter trip back to Westingtown was quiet, which gave Dasha time to think over what would happen once they reached her apartment.

Rordan knew she'd killed Dalton in self-defense. Was he

thinking about that now, how they'd be staying in a place where someone died?

He hadn't even been interested in meeting with anyone else who'd shared Omega-Three-Omega's experiences, opting to go straight to Dasha's apartment. She suspected it was more about getting away from Cecily than anything else, but she didn't press him on the subject. That could come later.

The biometric lock scanned Dasha's retina and opened with a near-silent hiss. Her apartment was as she'd left it the day before. If anyone else had come looking for her or Dalton, they hadn't left a trace.

Just to be sure, she checked her unit's security log from the wall-mounted monitor and breathed a small sigh of relief. No one had been in or out since she left with Cecily for the *Raider*.

"So, um, this is my home," she said, gesturing at the living room. A short hallway led to her bedroom and bathroom, and the rain-spattered plastiglas balcony doors let in some weak sunlight. "You can take my room if you want. I don't mind staying out here."

"I wouldn't put you out of your own bedroom," Rordan replied. "I'm used to much more spare accommodations."

The apartment was definitely spare by Dasha's standards. "I'm still not sure how long I'm staying here." Dasha sank down on the couch.

Rordan sat down next to her, his robe billowing a little around him. "Is it because of the water company that's after me?" he asked.

"Yeah. That, and my dad. They're after the one person in the galaxy who knows how to cybernetically enhance people."

"There's no one else who can?"

"There were two others, but they died."

"How?"

Dasha mulled over how to answer that. "Cecily killed

Garrett Jacoby, the doctor who enhanced you and the other men at Omega-Three-Omega," she said. "She was on a rescue mission with some of the other people who are now on Kurkay-2. The other one was Colton Byers, and he kept Serena—the woman you met on Cecily's ship—captive for something like ten years, making her this insanely advanced cyborg. I don't know the details. Serena doesn't talk about him much."

"Father Nelo spoke of justifiable deaths at the temple," said Rordan thoughtfully.

Dasha didn't want to get into a theological or philosophical discussion about justifiable homicide right now. "I assure you that Jacoby and Byers's deaths were necessary. I know I'm not the stars and God above, and I'm not supposed to be making those kinds of calls, but they were monsters. So was Janek Dalton. None of us are particularly proud of killing people, but it was them or us. It was Jacoby or you." She'd tried to keep the irritation out of her voice and doubted she was successful. "And it was Dalton or me, you, and my dad. He probably figured out a way to hack into a military roster to get your ident chip information. You came very close to being captured."

Exhaustion crashed over her, and she wanted nothing else in that moment but to take a shower and get some sleep.

"I've upset you," Rordan said. "And I haven't thanked you for saving me. I've been difficult and ungrateful since we met."

"You haven't. I'm just very tired. I imagine you are, too, and you don't have to thank me."

"I don't need much sleep."

"Right. Cyborg. Okay, I'm going to take a shower. You're welcome to, as well."

"I can get in the shower with you?"

Was that hope in his voice, or was Dasha more tired than she thought? Was he just cracking a joke?

Why did that idea sound appealing? She'd just met him, he'd lost his memory, and he was a novice monk in a religious order that embraced celibacy. Her face grew warm, and she knew she must be blushing furiously.

"Ha ha," she said, brushing it off. "I'll just be a few minutes, and then you can take your turn."

She bolted from the living room, hoping he hadn't noticed her flaming face.

CHAPTER 7

BROTHER RORDAN'S gaze alternated between the ceiling and living room window as he watched the gray morning unfurl itself through the curtain. He didn't have to get up from the couch to find out if the sun would be hidden by clouds, or if it would rain today. He could feel the imminent rain in his marrow, thought he could taste it in the air.

He and Dasha hadn't spoken much since they arrived at her apartment the day before. She'd slept a few hours the previous morning and spent much of the afternoon trying to engage in conversation with him. But he hadn't felt like delving into what he remembered of his past, instead preferring to meditate. And later, when she'd gone to bed for the night, he prayed, just as he did now as Westingtown started waking up.

The stars aren't answering.

Frustration welled up inside him. *Why am I facing this trial? What good could it come of it? I don't belong with these people.*

He closed his eyes and pictured Father Nelo. He knew what his superior would have said if he'd come to him with those questions: "Why *not* you?"

Brother Rordan used to believe that no one received more grief than one could handle. But as an unwelcome lump in his throat grew, he found himself questioning that belief.

I don't know if I can't do this, or I simply don't want to.

He thought about the woman who had saved him and probably the entire temple, had taken him into her home and how she added another layer of complication to his life.

A novice monk shouldn't be intrigued by a woman he'd just met. Or any women, for that matter.

She may not be an angel, but she was sent to help me.

His breath stilled, and a welcome sense of peace descended on him.

Had that been the answer to his prayers all along? Was Dasha herself the answer?

Brother Rordan considered it. True, his life had been forever upended from the second he found her in the river, but she'd had a solution to every challenge his cyborg status presented, including the promise of a life-saving surgery that could be performed by her very own father.

And I turned it down!

He felt like an idiot. He should've listened to Dasha and her father, had the surgery, and then he would be that much closer to figuring out what to do next, without having to worry about something in his head that could go off at any moment and kill him.

He relaxed a little under the blanket. He could still have the procedure. Dr. Caron had been eager to do it yesterday; surely, his mind hadn't changed in such a short time frame.

Brother Rordan couldn't will himself back to sleep, but he could relax a little. Propped up by pillows against the couch's armrest, some of the tension left his body. He thought he might be closer to an answer as to what God, the universe, and the stars expected from him, and that answer included Dasha.

Rordan was awake and sitting at the kitchen table when Dasha woke up, his eyes closed in prayer. She moved as quietly as she could, fetching a tea cube and hot water from the dispenser built into the wall, not wanting to disturb him.

No such luck. "Good morning," he said, a serene smile on his face.

"Good morning. Don't mind me," she said.

"It's your home. Move around as you please."

"Will do. Have you had breakfast?" She opened a cupboard and took out a package of dehydrated scones. She popped them in the food processor and set it to rehydrate them.

"I didn't feel right poking around your things."

"Go ahead. There isn't that much to poke around in. Want a scone?"

Rordan finally opened his eyes, and she saw an expression of peace there that she'd never been subjected to before. Aside from the slight glow in his eyes, he looked every bit the calm, collected monk she knew he strived to be.

"No, thank you," he said. "I'm willing to have that surgery as soon as possible if your father will still agree to it."

A wave of relief crashed over Dasha. "Oh, thank God," she said.

"I beg your pardon?"

"The stars!" she corrected herself. "Thank the stars and universe. And God, I guess. All of them." The processor pinged, but she scarcely noticed it. "You have no idea how much I was hoping you'd change your mind. My dad's going to be so happy to hear that."

He nodded. "I prayed over it, and while the stars chose not to be explicit with their intentions for me, my head is clearer. I have direction and purpose."

Dasha didn't care how he came to the conclusion that life-saving surgery was the way to go, only that he'd done it. "Dad's going to be so relieved to hear that," she said. "And when Jason Formosa had his surgery, he was up and about and back to normal in a couple of hours."

Would seeing his fellow cyborg-in-arms trigger his old memories?

She'd received messages on her thincomp from her friends and acquaintances since yesterday, all of them asking after Rordan. Valenna Merchant and Anders Barris, in particular, were quite worried about him, and Dasha wanted Rordan to meet them as soon as possible. Of everyone who'd been on Omega-Three-Omega, Anders was the most knowledgeable, and as far as they knew, the cyborg who'd undergone the most experiments. He'd been trapped on that hellhole longer than any of them.

She slid the food processor's flap open and took out the package of scones. They smelled good, but it was deceptive. Rehydrated scones always tasted a little off, a strange combination of sweet and stale. She missed her oven and the real food she'd enjoyed in Princess Cay.

"Well, I'm glad to hear you have a purpose," she said. "Although I'm sure you always did. I'll send a message to my dad, and we'll get in a flitter and go back to Anders and Valenna's property as soon as possible."

She took a fortifying sip of tea, then a bite from a rehydrated scone. *Ugh.* She didn't have any butter or even butter substitute on hand to take the edge off the taste.

She forced it down and swallowed more tea. Maybe Valenna had something better in her kitchen, or the lounge's replicator on the *Gray Ghost* could kick out something more edible. "Let me get dressed," she said. "And then we'll be on our way."

Stars and the universe be praised!

Brother Rordan had made it aboard the *Gray Ghost*, and he hadn't seen a single soul on the ship aside from the kindly Dr. Caron. The anxiety he'd been holding over the possibility of seeing Cecily Barris again dissipated, and he lay down on the ship's diag bed with a sense of lightness he hadn't expected to feel.

"This is straightforward," Dr. Caron said. "I have your specs from the blueprints Cecily took from Omega-Three-Omega. Your enhancements are much more sophisticated than your counterparts there, which is why I suspect you didn't die after you dug out your military ident chip. That was a stupid thing to do, by the way."

Brother Rordan met Dr. Caron's gaze, but he didn't see condemnation there despite the physician's words. "I was worried about putting Dasha in danger," he said. "If she could find me so easily, what would keep someone with more advanced technology?"

"A worthy goal, and one I approve of," Dr. Caron said. "But if you didn't have the nanobots you have, you would have died immediately. You're closer to Serena Glazer, cyborg-wise, than Jason." He looked up at the ceiling. "Please excuse me. I shouldn't be speaking about patients that way, but..."

"These are extenuating circumstances," Brother Rordan said.

"Yes, although I should still remember patient confidentiality. You and the other cyborgs used to be very open with each other over a shared broadcast link, but that doesn't mean it's all right for me to abandon my medical ethics."

Broadcast link?

Brother Rordan's body went rigid.

A memory came back, slamming into him.

He and a group of other men, working outside in the cold as they repaired something or other. Wind and freezing rain whipped by their faces, and they were powerless to do anything about it as they methodically patched damaged equipment back together.

But were they powerless? Brother Rordan had the impression that they were obeying someone's orders out of fear, that if they refused to work, they would be physically punished.

An electric shock. *He'd experienced it before, once. His whole body unable to move, his eyes unable to blink, as an unending wave of electricity bolted through him, searing every nerve ending. He thought he would die.*

And if he didn't complete this repair, he would experience it again. The shock was a million times worse than the below-freezing temperature he worked in.

And then there was a new voice calling into his mind: "This is Captain Barris of the Gray Ghost. *I've received your SOS. Sit tight, I have help on the way."*

"Brother Rordan?"

He snapped back to the present. Dr. Caron waited patiently. Maybe he'd known Brother Rordan was gripped in the throes of a flashback.

"Everything okay?" the doctor asked.

"Yes." He blinked, Cecily's words echoing in his mind.

She'd been there to help him. She hadn't been able to save everyone, but she'd tried. And according to Dr. Caron, to Dasha, she'd taken his medical information to help him further. He needed to cut her a little slack.

Except for the cargo hold. He would never go down there again if he could help it.

"I'm fine, Doctor," Brother Rordan said. He tried to force a smile to his face and hoped it was convincing. "Let's do this."

Dasha sat at Valenna's kitchen table, clutching a mug of rapidly cooling tea in an effort to keep her hands from shaking. Her throat clogged, and her eyes burned with unshed tears, a couple of them falling and landing on the tabletop in tiny splatters.

Now that she was in her friend's home, away from the distraction Rordan provided, the horror of what had happened in her apartment days before weighed on her. When a sniffle escaped her, Valenna's arm wrapped around her, and Dasha leaned into her, needing the contact.

"Janek Dalton was a monster," Valenna said softly. "He had no qualms about hurting or killing you to get what he wanted. You did what you had to do to stay alive."

"I don't know how Cecily does it," Dasha said, voice watery.

"You're not quite in the same league as Cecily. And I know she doesn't talk about it much, but when it really hit Serena after she killed Colton Byers, she was nearly inconsolable. And that fucker *deserved* to die, too."

Dasha wiped at her eyes and nodded. She had a bare knowledge of the facts surrounding Serena's imprisonment on an uninhabited moon in the Zone. Serena had killed the man who bought her from her parents when she was a kid.

"I can't believe I was able to sleep there," Dasha said. "I think having Rordan there helped."

"Do you think you'll be able to sleep there again tonight?"

"I don't know."

"You're welcome to stay here," Valenna said. "Now that Cressida and Lukas have their own place, we have the room."

Dasha considered it. "Rordan might like that. I think he likes communing with nature and physical labor."

"We wouldn't make him work. Or you." Valenna took a

seat next to Dasha. "You've been through something traumatic, and you need to get away for a bit. Or you could get a whole new apartment and start over there."

Dasha had thought about that, briefly, when she went to bed last night. But she knew the memories of Dalton would haunt her somewhere else, too. All the apartments in Westingtown were identical; the only thing that would change for her was the view outside the windows. No, as long as she had to live on Kurkay-2, she'd remember Dalton. She would probably think about him every day until she could go back home to Princess Cay.

Homesickness gripped her heart when she thought about the treehouse she and her dad shared. She fiercely missed it and her students.

"I'll think about it," Dasha finally said. "Thank you for the offer." But even as she said the words, she already knew that spending a few days with Valenna and Anders wouldn't solve anything. It would only prolong the strange grief that held her.

"I'm not an expert on anything," Valenna said. "But I do know that you have to cut yourself some slack when something terrible has happened."

Dasha didn't want to talk about Dalton anymore and changed the subject. "I just wish Rordan remembered why he went to Spaceport 44 in the first place," Dasha said. "And what was done to him."

"If anyone can figure out what happened to him there, it'll be your dad," Valenna said. "Or possibly Serena, if she's up to doing any hacking, which she probably isn't for the time being."

Or maybe Rordan would eventually remember on his own, even though he didn't want to. Dasha could only hope that if and when his memories came rushing back, he didn't back down from them.

Brother Rordan said a silent prayer to the stars and universe as he lay down on the diag bed in the *Gray Ghost*'s sickbay. A selfish part of him desperately hoped that a sense of calmness would be bestowed on him during Dr. Caron's surgery, but as the doctor dipped his hands in a blue sterilizing solution, he knew his pleas were in vain.

Or the universe was testing his strength.

He's really going to cut my head open!

The memory of Father Nelo's voice sounded in his head: "We are not tested. The stars already know your strength and do not engage in such foolishness for the sake of your suffering."

Blue glove solution.

Brother Rordan had seen that before. Blue hands, ready to open him up and turn him into a monster, something he'd agreed to for money. *Money! What good is it?*

Another man who'd used the title of "Doctor" had pulled him open, planted what he'd called "nanobots" in his body. Another memory resurfaced, as quick as a fish's fin breaking the surface of a lake before disappearing again, the condescending voice of the doctor saying, "This is the most advanced technology in the universe. A colleague developed it. You're a good candidate for these enhancements, Captain Alexander, given your education. Your counterparts with metal sticking out of their bodies can't say the same."

My education?

Before he could ruminate on that further, another memory of blue hands surfaced, but this time in a grimy room, and the same gravelly voiced man who attached his syntho-skin: "I've never seen so many nanobots in one body before."

Blue solution-dipped hands. Oh, stars, why are you doing this to me? Why am I doing this to myself?

He couldn't focus on Dr. Caron's soothing voice or think about his and Dasha's reassurances that he would be okay after this was done, that he might have a chance at living a life he wanted after his kill switch was deactivated.

Dasha's beautiful.

She was kind, she was caring. She'd put her fears about her home, her residual terror after she had to kill someone to save herself, aside for him.

Maybe she's a different kind of angel than the celestial.

Was it fair that the universe literally dropped her in front of him when he was preparing to take his monk's vows? Or was there another purpose for him?

His spiritual ruminations, as brief a distraction as they were from the terror that the sight of Dr. Caron's blue hands induced in him, evaporated as his body went slack and his mind blank.

CHAPTER 8

DASHA COULDN'T FOCUS on the musical vid unfolding in front of her. She appreciated Valenna and Cressida's attempt to take her mind off Rordan, still recovering aboard the *Gray Ghost*, but she couldn't bring herself to care about the plight of the couple caterwauling at each other across Cressida's thincomp screen.

It's been four hours. Dad hasn't got in touch.

Was that a good sign? How long was Jason out after having his brain surgery?

I really hate musicals. I don't get what Cressida sees in them.

She sneaked a glance at Valenna, whose eyes had glazed over in boredom. Dasha wasn't the only one who didn't care about the vid.

But Cressida had a dreamy look on her face as she watched the show, even though it was probably one she'd seen a dozen times before. "This is one of Lukas's favorites," she confided to them.

Just when she thought she wouldn't be able to stand it anymore, the front door opened with a noisy bang. All three of them shot to their feet, trailing behind Valenna. "Anders?" she called. "Lukas?"

They came to a stop in the foyer where Rordan stood, outlined by the cloud-filtered sunlight streaming in through the open door. Between the light haloing his close-cropped dark hair and his blue novice monk's robe, he looked like a divine entity. Dasha's heart stopped at the sight, and she found herself momentarily speechless.

Behind him was her father, who did *not* look pleased. "I told him to lie down," Dr. Caron said helplessly.

"I don't need to," Rordan said.

There was something different about his voice. While there was always a steely resoluteness in his tone, it was still gentle. Warm. Quiet. Exactly the sort of voice a monk would need if he wanted to be a source of comfort to the distressed or infirm.

Now, his voice held an edge of authority, and it was louder. More commanding. For the first time, Dasha could understand how the man was once a soldier.

"Dasha." Rordan spoke her name with an authority she hadn't heard before. His determined gaze locked with hers, and she suppressed a shiver that hadn't derived from fear.

It took a few seconds for her to find her voice. "Brother Rordan? Dad? How did the surgery go?" She immediately felt like an idiot. If he was standing, alive, before her, clearly it was successful.

"Just 'Rordan' is fine," he replied, his voice clipped.

Dasha looked at her father, who had moved between them. Now a ripple of fear coursed through her. *Is he protecting me from him?*

"Did you get your memory back?" she asked. Dimly, she was aware of Cressida behind her, of her friend's reassuring hand on her shoulder. Or maybe she was trying to protect her, too.

Rordan closed his eyes for a few seconds, as if in prayer. Dasha didn't know she was holding her breath until he replied, "Part of it."

"And your kill switch is deactivated?" Her eyes shifted between him and Dr. Caron.

"It was already deactivated," Rordan said. "It never worked in the first place, according to this good doctor here."

She wasn't as surprised as she thought she would be over such a revelation; none of the cyborgs, to her knowledge, had much in common in the way of their enhancements. All of them were unique. "How?" she asked.

"Rordan's cybernetics are closer to Serena's than the others," Dr. Caron said. "He isn't tied to a particular ecosystem the way she originally was, so it appears that Garrett Jacoby improved on Colton Byers's technology. They're also the only two cyborgs without ocular data readouts, all the better to blend in."

"I'm pumped full of nanobots," Rordan said bitterly. "And they can't be removed. I'm going to be like this forever."

"You can still be a monk," she said. "The Great Faith acknowledges that no one is unredeemable by the grace of the stars, doesn't it?" To her knowledge, at least.

A tiny shake of his head was his only response.

Valenna spoke up. "What you did before you were a monk doesn't define who you are now," she said quietly. "God and the stars know I certainly have. Positive change is possible."

Rordan blinked as if finally noticing Valenna for the first time. "I remember you," he said.

Valenna didn't flinch. "I remember you, too."

"It was cold outside," he said. "Snowing. You were disembarking a freighter and weren't dressed for the weather."

"Yeah," said Valenna.

"I was with someone," Rordan said. "I remember when he died in the ship's hold."

"Bell, yeah." There was a catch in her voice. "You two brought me to the base on Omega-Three-Omega when I was tricked into taking a job there."

Something in Rordan's expression shuttered at Valenna's words, and he didn't reply to her. To Dr. Caron, he asked, "Is my procedure over with?"

"Yes. But I'd still prefer it if I could keep an eye on you for a while longer."

"No. You told me yourself that I have nanobots running through me that are keeping me alive. I'd prefer to convalesce away from that ship."

"Okay," said Dasha. "We'll go back to my apartment if you want."

"Dasha," said Dr. Caron, a note of warning in his voice.

"I'm not going to kill your daughter," Rordan snapped.

Dasha thought she might have felt everyone in the foyer flinching simultaneously. "I wasn't worried about that," she said.

"I wouldn't touch a hair on her head," Rordan continued. "She's..." He paused as if he hadn't wanted to finish the sentence. "I wouldn't hurt any of you."

"The flitter's out back," Dasha said. "Let me get it, and we'll go back if you want."

"Are you sure you don't want to talk to Anders or Jason?" Valenna asked. "Or Lukas? They're working on the ground apple orchard we're cultivating here. I can call them, and they'll be back in a few minutes. You're welcome here."

"I'm not ready for that yet," Rordan said. "Eventually. I need to lie down like the good doctor suggested, and I need to think some things over."

He sounded less anxious, but Dasha didn't know how long that would last.

"I appreciate the invitation," Rordan added. "But give me some time."

The look he sent Dasha's way was almost beseeching, and she saw the message underneath it: "Get me out of here."

She nodded. "Let's go."

After hugging her friends goodbye, Dr. Caron walked with her and Rordan outside to where the flitter waited. Before she could board it, her father took her elbow and whispered, "I don't think this is a good idea, but keep an eye on him. Notify me immediately if you see any change in his behavior."

"I can already see a change in his behavior," she said.

If Rordan could hear their conversation—and she was sure he could, with his enhanced hearing—he gave no indication of it. He let himself into the flitter with surprising grace and waited.

"If you notice anything alarming," Dr. Caron amended, frustration edging into his voice. "God damn it, Dasha. I worry about him becoming violent."

Her mind drifted back to the last time a man became violent in her home, and she shuddered. "I doubt that'll happen," she protested, but worry slithered into her mind over the possibility.

Was she making a gigantic mistake?

But the look Rordan gave her, full of patience and understanding, settled her nerves.

"We'll be fine, Dad," she said. "When do you want him to come back for a checkup?"

"Tomorrow or the day after," he said. "I'd prefer it if he'd agree to stay aboard the *Gray Ghost*, but he refuses to. Even though Serena could answer some of his questions about nanobots better than I could."

"How is she doing?"

"I think the baby's going to arrive a little early, but she's fine otherwise. She's up and walking and tired of being pregnant."

Dasha smiled and hugged Dr. Caron. "Let me know as soon as she goes into labor," she said. "We're all excited to meet little Serena or Matthias."

"I will. Take care, sweetheart. Stay safe."

———

The trip back to her Westingtown apartment was quiet, but tension radiated from Rordan in silent waves. She saw his fists clench and relax a few times, and he looked like he wanted to say something, but he didn't.

He would talk to her about his memories when he was ready, if at all. Dasha just wanted to be his friend.

It wasn't until they returned to her apartment when he said, "I remember parts of the war."

Dasha had just toed off her rain boots and froze in the foyer. "You do?"

She followed Rordan to the living room, where he sank into the couch, still draped in his blankets from the night before. "That was the first thing I remembered after I came to after the surgery," he said. There was an uncertainty to his voice like he was trying to piece together his memories as he went along. She sat next to him and waited for him to continue.

If he wanted to continue.

He was quiet for so long that Dasha thought it might be prudent for her to leave him alone.

"I remember one battle in particular, but I'm not sure when it happened. My unit planted signal disruptors on a Bravan spaceport's exterior docking bay doors, and I think... I think they shut off the air."

Shame laced his words, and beneath it, an undercurrent of anger and self-loathing.

"You did that under orders," Dasha began, but he cut her off.

"It doesn't matter," he said bitterly. "The Bravans on that station are just as dead as if I'd thought to attach those disruptors myself. I'm still complicit. I'm still a murderer." His hands balled into fists, and she suspected that if he had less self-control, he would have planted one of them through her coffee table.

"And yet they *still* opened the border to Zone refugees," he said. "Even though they knew that Zone was trying to encroach on their territory, force them to adapt to their ways and privatize every single resource they had and make their citizens for things like air and water, they still let us settle here."

"The Bravans differentiate between the average Zone citizen and their totalitarian government," Dasha said. "They knew who to look out for when they opened the border to resettlement. I'm sure they had ident chip records of every person who emigrated."

The memory of Janek Dalton resurfaced, and she closed her eyes for a second, fighting back a wave of nausea. She'd killed him in this very room.

How had he managed to slip over the border? He probably wasn't as important to the underworld as Dasha thought if he hadn't been turned away.

He took the bounty, remember. He had powerful people after him, people who are still looking for Rordan.

But he didn't seem to be listening. "I killed their citizens," Rordan said, more to himself. "And they still let me cross over the border."

"Do you remember crossing it at all?" she asked, hoping the question wasn't too forward.

"No," he said abruptly. "And I don't want to remember it

right now, and if we talk about it, I'm afraid it'll come back. I need some time to process everything." He stood up and walked to the balcony doors, looking out at the sparsely populated street below them. "I need to pray for the souls of the people I killed. I have to pray for their forgiveness and that of the stars, not that I deserve it." He faced Dasha, then looked down at his robe again, disgust written across his face. "I don't deserve to wear this, either."

"You do," Dasha pleaded. "I don't remember a lot about the Zone, but I know most people don't have a lot of choice in whether they join the military or not. You did what you had to do in order to live. And it was *war*."

This time, when her tears threatened again, she didn't fight them. She brushed them away impatiently, heart aching for the man before her who had, once again, lost everything he held dear.

"Is there a Great Faith temple in Westingtown?" he asked.

"There's nothing yet for any religion on Kurkay-2," she replied, wishing she had better news for him.

"It's no matter," Rordan said. "I'm not fit to show my face in a temple. I'll pray here if that's all right with you."

"Yeah." She stood up. "Do you want a cookie or tea or something?" Trying to read his expression, she added, "Just... I'm not that familiar with monks' etiquette."

"Will you stay with me?"

The question surprised her, and she found herself saying, "Yeah, of course."

Rordan kneeled on the carpet, facing the balcony. "You don't have to pray if you don't want to. I'm going to say mine silently. But I'd like it if you waited with me."

Dasha crossed the short distance between the couch and the balcony doors and assumed the same position next to him. She didn't know what to say.

But he surprised her again, wrapping his hand around hers, and lowering his head, eyes closed. Outside, the clouds parted just long enough to let bright sunshine spill across the room.

CHAPTER 9

ONCE AGAIN, Rordan found himself wide awake in the middle of the night, stretched out on Dasha's couch, unable to sleep.

But now he understood why, that it wasn't just his thoughts running overtime.

I don't have to sleep. I don't need it anymore.

He wished desperately that he could sleep because he knew that whatever dreams or nightmares the stars threw at him couldn't be worse than the memories that wouldn't stop resurfacing.

Like his childhood home on Garshan, far too large for only him and his parents.

I guess I had family money? I remember my parents being proud that only the best lived there.

I wish I'd died on Omega-Three-Omega or in the Gray Ghost*'s hold. It would've made things so much easier for me.*

Wishing death upon oneself was sacrilege according to the holy books he'd read, but he couldn't keep himself from feeling that way. Only his prayers and meditation earlier in the day, with Dasha's hand in his own, had offered him any semblance of comfort.

Something in him warmed when he thought of her, sleeping only a few meters away.

She wasn't Father Nelo or a follower of the Great Faith, but she was a kind person and fortifying presence. Out of everyone he'd met so far on Kurkay-2, Dasha was the only person he truly worried about putting in danger from the water company after him.

But if they stayed together, he could protect her. And unlike the other monks at the Glissat temple, she wouldn't judge him for his old life. She wasn't a believer, but she still espoused the values of kindness and compassion the Great Faith commanded of its adherents.

He needed to learn more about himself, find out why he'd lost his memory, and what led him to seek out such a procedure in the first place. How Rordan Alexander, the soldier, would have handled the mess he was in.

A plan formed in his mind, one that, prior to his arrival on Kurkay-2, he never would have considered.

He shucked off the blanket and stood up, then paced around the short length of the living room, thinking about how to execute his idea.

He might be beyond divine intervention, but he could still save Dasha.

***

"Dasha."

Dasha snuggled deeper into her pillows and blankets, not wanting her dream featuring Rordan to end.

"Dasha." There was his voice again, less sexy than it was a few minutes ago and more insistent.

Oh, shit.

She jerked fully awake and saw the star of her dream, its memory rapidly fading away, crouched next to her bed. She felt herself blush when his metallic-tinged eyes met hers, and she sat up, wrapping the blankets around herself.

"Good morning," she said. "Is everything okay?"

Rordan hesitated. "I've made a decision about my life."

She had the feeling he was going to say something she wasn't going to like. "What?"

"I think it's best for everyone if I leave Kurkay-2," he said.

It took a couple of seconds for the weight of his words to have an impact. "What?" Dasha repeated. She threw off the covers and got out of bed, nearly crashing into him in the process. "No," she said. "No, you need to stay here."

"I can't," he said.

"If this is about your guilt about the war, we can help you," she said. "My dad can help you. The other cyborgs are willing to, as well. But it's best if you stay here."

"I'm a walking target until that water corporation shows up," said Rordan. "That bounty hunter was looking for me in particular. I was thinking about it last night, and it's probably because I'm the cyborg likeliest to pass for strictly human. They don't have any interest in the others because they have more visible cybernetic features, and I doubt they know Serena exists since she spent her life cloistered away. And if they did, her nanobots don't work."

Dasha's shock ebbed just enough so she could focus on what he was saying. It made sense. Aside from his eyes, and the ports in his wrists, there wasn't a single feature that marked him as a cyborg. The others had more scarring from their surgeries, more visible ports in their necks, and in Lukas's case, his black gloves that kept his hands from turning into instruments of death.

"I have to leave," Rordan continued. "I need to find answers about myself, and I don't think they'll come through prayer alone."

She heard the pain in his voice when he spoke about

prayer, and with it, an ache corresponded in her heart. "Where would you go?"

He looked away for a few seconds.

"Rordan?" she said. "What half-assed plan have you come up with?"

"Nothing half-assed," he replied. "I have a couple of ideas, none of which involve returning to Glissat and endangering the other monks there. Not that I could hide there, anyway. I won't risk them."

"You won't risk us," Dasha protested. "Stay here. If you don't feel right about staying in my apartment, you could stay with Valenna and Anders, or Cressida and Lukas."

He shook his head. "No. I came here to say goodbye and thank you, and I'll be off."

"No," she said. "You can't go." As if to further drive her point home, she grabbed his arm. "Stay with me."

She'd never demanded a man stay with her before, and she didn't know what possessed her now. All that mattered was keeping him safe until Wilton Intergalactic Fluid Technology could be deterred.

But she couldn't force him to do what she thought was best. He was in his situation because other people thought they had the right to control him.

She immediately let go of him, letting her hand drop at her side.

Rordan looked startled at the lack of contact, but she didn't touch him again.

She tried another tack, one she hoped would help him see reason. "If you want to take off," she said, "I'm coming with you."

Something in his expression shifted, grew a little... warmer, maybe? Happier?

"I'd love it if you did," he replied.

And Dasha knew, by the hope in his voice, that he would call her bluff.

God damn it.

———

Half an hour later, Dasha struggled to keep up with Rordan as he strode through her apartment complex to the outside flitter pavilion. Kurkay-2's perpetual rain lightly fell to the ground, but Dasha didn't care about that.

She had to make him change his mind about leaving.

He helped her into one of the flitters, and surprised her when he sat at the control panel. "You used your thumbprint to start this yesterday," he said. "I won't have any problem navigating the flitter, but I doubt it has any of my biometrics on file."

Dasha sighed, wishing she'd tried harder to talk him out of leaving her apartment, and pressed her thumb to the print reader on the control panel. The flitter immediately started, and Rordan expertly guided it away from the pavilion to the main road.

"You should've brought a bag," he said.

"At least I'm dressed, and I cleaned my teeth." He wasn't really going to go through with taking off, was he?

Her trepidation increased as the flitter sped along the street, still empty in the early morning, all the way to the public shipyard where the *Dragonfly*, the small ship belonging to Adam Johnston and Esme Hammond, was housed. The trepidation turned into near full-blown panic when she watched Rordan expertly place his hand on the exterior palm lock, where it whirred longer than it should have before it finally unlocked. The passenger airlock door opened with a hydraulic hiss.

The import of what he was doing hit her full-force. "Does Adam know you're stealing his ship?" Dasha demanded.

"I'm borrowing it," replied Rordan. He reached for her hand. "And I'm borrowing it for a good reason."

God damn it, why did that small motion have to feel so good? He was a cyborg and a novice monk who still wasn't sure who he really was, and they hardly knew each other. Why did she want to go with him? What was it about Rordan that compelled her to follow him?

None of it made sense, but little in her life had made sense since Jason and Cecily turned up at her home on Sidra Prime, weeks ago, looking for life-saving surgery from her father.

"Where are you going, and why?" she asked. "Tell me that much, and I'll come with you."

He paused as if warring with himself about answering. "Spaceport 44," he finally said. "I have a feeling a lot of the answers I need will be found there."

She'd suggested as much before, and he'd denied it. "You want to go to the Zone? Are you fucking insane?" She tried to jerk her hand away, but he didn't let go. "We're going home," she said. "This is nuts." She tried to pull him away, but he was like a rock.

"If I stay here, I'm going to put everyone in danger," Rordan said. His voice was low and dangerous, a tone she'd never heard before. "It's not just the other cyborgs. It's everyone else in Westingtown, the whole planet. And it's you."

Her breath caught. She tried to speak and failed.

"If you stay with me, I can keep you safe," he said.

Her mind flashed back to their meeting in the river, and him carrying her out of the water with such care. She'd been freaked out to all hell when that happened, but once she realized where she was and who he was, she'd felt protected, too, in a weird way. Even though he was an adherent to a peaceful religion.

Was he abandoning the Great Faith now?

I must be losing my mind. Either that or I just don't want to let go of him.

He could get himself killed if he went to the Zone alone.

Indecision warred within her until she heard herself say, "I might regret this later, but okay. Let's go."

As he prepped the *Dragonfly* for takeoff, Rordan mulled over the events of the morning in his mind.

He was stealing a ship. And it wasn't just any ship, but one that belonged to someone he was trapped on Omega-Three-Omega with. Someone who was allegedly his friend. His not remembering his former comrade wasn't an excuse.

Dasha squeaked in surprise when the *Dragonfly*'s engines engaged, and she began a rocky ascent. "You're really doing this!" she yelped. She grabbed the back of the pilot's seat to steady herself as she looked around the barebones cockpit. There wasn't a copilot's seat, which struck Rordan as odd.

"Oh, my God," she said. "I can't believe you're actually stealing Adam and Esme's ship. I didn't think you would."

His hands seemed to move of their own accord as he set a course for the Zone, and from there, Spaceport 44.

I know the course! I know how to fly a ship!

Muscle memory was an incredible thing.

He stopped thinking about it when the ship's heavy air engine kicked in with a groan louder than he liked, with a jolt hard enough to send Dasha sprawling across him. "Damn it!" she said, voice muffled.

The *Dragonfly* hit Kurkay-2's atmosphere as she struggled to right herself, and the ship's antiquated heavy air engine made fighting with gravity almost impossible. Dasha seemed to give up and lay against him, chest pressed to his, her face against his shoulder. Her hair tickled his cheek.

Oh, this is not good.

The position set off a riot of vaguely familiar sensations and reactions roaring through his body, ones he dearly hoped Dasha didn't notice while the *Dragonfly* fought Kurkay-2's gravity. All of his thoughts about Spaceport 44 evaporated, the moral misgivings he'd harbored about stealing the *Dragonfly* forgotten, and all he and his traitorous body could focus on was the woman stuck against him.

His mind flashed back to their first meeting when he thought she was an angel. He still hadn't fully discounted that possibility, even if angels weren't supposed to be sexy.

He shifted a little, praying that Dasha would think he was fighting gravity, too. He tried to remember the Edicts of the Stars, the first thing he learned when he joined the Glissat monks, but could only recall the first words of the First Edict: "Praise be to God, the universe and stars, without whom none of their children would exist." He recited them a couple of times in his mind and thought he finally had a handle on his body's reactions.

Then the *Dragonfly* broke atmosphere with a final hurdle, shattering his concentration.

At least the heavy air engine went silent, and the ship's gravity went back to normal. Dasha peeled herself away from Rordan and stood up on legs that wobbled a little. She stared at the forward viewscreen, at the image of Kurkay-2 before them. "I can't believe you actually stole a ship," she said. She turned around to face Rordan. "I can't believe *we* stole a ship. We should go back!"

Rordan had already plotted a course for the Zone-Bravan border, and he had no intention of returning to Kurkay-2 now. "No."

"This is the stupidest thing I've ever done," Dasha said. "I can't believe I went along with it. I can't believe I'm trapped on a ship *again*, and I didn't think the reason could possibly be stupider than last time."

"You were willing to come here with me," Rordan pointed out.

"I didn't think you were serious!" she said. "And if you were, I thought maybe I could talk you out of it."

"Monks are men of their words."

"I'm not religious," she said, her tone surprisingly calm. He suspected it was the voice she used with unruly children in the classroom. "I respect your right to be, but I don't follow the Great Faith at all. And the way Jason talks about how he grew up with it, it didn't sound that great."

"Adherents in the Zone are known to be fundamentalists."

"They are." She rubbed her eyes, and he could see the tension in the motion, feel her frustration. For a few seconds, guilt chewed at his conscience.

"Can we get in touch with everyone, at least?" she asked. "Let them know we're okay, and you haven't snapped and kidnapped me?"

Rordan's hands froze over the command console. He hadn't considered the possibility of being accused of kidnapping.

"Of course," he said. "We'll do that right away."

"And we're going to return this ship to Adam and Esme in one piece, right?" she pressed. "We're taking a quick trip to that spaceport and coming right back home before anyone realizes we're in the Zone."

He nodded. "Yes."

"And that's not just a cover story," she said. "We'll be back sooner rather than later."

An unfamiliar wave of irritation crested through him, and he bit back a sharp reply. *Tranquility and kindness, Rordan. Remember them.*

But he had the impression that he hadn't always had those qualities before he lost his memory and joined the temple.

There's no better reason to reconcile the positive traits I picked up at the temple with the military efficiency I seem to have grown up with.

He turned to face Dasha, who stood in the cockpit's doorway. Her full lips were set in a straight line, arms crossed under her breasts, as she stared at him.

He should turn the ship around right now, take her back to Kurkay-2 and relative safety. Except that the last time she was supposed to be protected by the other cyborgs, Janek Dalton broke into her apartment.

"I think being with me is the least-dangerous thing for you," he said finally.

"I'd ask if you really think you have the right to decide that for me, but I'm the one who followed you aboard this ship," she replied.

"And it isn't the other cyborgs that water company is after," Rordan said. "It's me."

"My father, too," Dasha said.

"I'm not so sure about that. He didn't design me, Garrett Jacoby did."

"No one designed you," she said. "Except maybe the stars. Jacoby just pumped you full of nanobots."

A warm, fuzzy feeling spread through him at her mention of the stars. His wavering spiritual beliefs aside, it pleased him to know she still respected his faith.

"It's selfish of me to feel this way," he said. He took a deep breath, fortifying himself and hoping what he was about to say wouldn't upset her too badly. His words came out in an uncharacteristic rush. "I wanted to keep you with me."

He wasn't supposed to feel the way he did; monks were supposed to eschew physical attraction. And until Dasha fell from the sky into the river, he'd been completely comfortable with the notion of lifelong celibacy.

She was bright and kind and beautiful. She could've easily manipulated him when he thought she was an angel to get him to go along with her, but she didn't. She'd been nothing but honest and helpful to him, and he'd stolen her from her family and friends for his own selfish reasons.

Her only reply to his confession was a shocked expression. She opened her mouth as if to say something, then thought better of it and closed it. Dasha turned away from him and walked away from the cockpit, her footsteps echoing along the corridor.

CHAPTER 10

ANXIETY WRACKED through Valenna's body as she thought best how to tell Anders, Cressida, and Lukas about the message she'd just received.

Oh, God. I have to face Dr. Caron, too.

Once upon a time, she would've worried about blame for being the messenger of it, and she had to remind herself she wasn't lost in Center City's drug dens again. No one was going to punish her for telling them that one Rordan Alexander, novice monk and reluctant cyborg, had stolen a ship.

But that wasn't even the worst part of it. He'd taken Dasha, too. And while Dasha was the one to give her the news and copious apologies for the worry and the "borrowing" of the *Dragonfly*, Valenna fretted about her most of all.

Dasha told her that she'd be in touch with her father, Adam, and Esme to explain what happened. She sounded reasonably calm in her recorded message, but its accompanying images of her—shadows under her eyes, a pinched look at the corners of her mouth that hadn't been there before—betrayed the tone in her voice.

Valenna left the house, her thincomp in hand, and

marched to the barn where she knew Anders and Lukas were working.

Their voices were light and carefree over the sound of nails being hammered into wood: they were building another pen for the new goats Anders wanted to buy. A chill slithered through Valenna when she thought of goats, and for a few seconds, she forgot about Dasha and Rordan.

Where the fuck is Dolly?

The goat they already had absolutely loathed Valenna and took any and all opportunities to chase her or headbutt her. She didn't know what she'd done to offend the creature, but she avoided her all the same. She nervously cast a few looks around the barn, hoping she wasn't about to be assaulted.

She didn't hear so much as a bleat. She relaxed a little. *Maybe the bitch has decided to just eat the beron nuts I planted, instead.*

"Anders?" she called. "Lukas?"

Their chatter and the sound of hammering ceased as she walked to the back of the barn. "Everything okay?" Anders asked. "And look out for Dolly. She's in the stall next to you."

Valenna jumped, expecting to be headbutted, but the stall's door was closed. When looked into it, she saw the godforsaken goat, her kid next to her. Dolly let out a bleat that Valenna thought might've been her version of a growl.

Ugh. Valenna held out her thincomp. "Something bad's happened," she said.

"Oh, shit," said Anders, just as Lukas said, "Is it Cressida?"

"Cressida's fine," said Valenna. Her sister had left earlier to pick up a few things from the Westingtown market and would be back soon. "It's Rordan and Dasha."

She rested her thincomp on the stall's edge and activated Dasha's message. By the time it was over, Anders and Lukas wore expressions of shock and anger.

Valenna glanced between them, trying to gauge their reactions. "So, what do we do?" she asked in a small voice.

"Something rational," Anders said, an edge to his voice. "As much as I'd love to hop aboard the *Gray Ghost* and find out what the hell Rordan was thinking, we have to think about Dasha's safety. Something might have snapped in him. We don't want him to take it out on her."

"I don't think he'd do that," Valenna protested. "He's a monk."

"Monks don't usually steal things, either," Lukas said.

Well, way to make me feel stupid, Lukas. "What I meant is, he wouldn't hurt Dasha," said Valenna. "I think he cares about her."

Why else would he bring her along on his joyride? The way Rordan looked at Dasha hadn't escaped Valenna's notice. Rordan might not realize it, and Dasha probably didn't either, but there was a simmering heat in his metallic eyes that had been unmistakable to Valenna. She'd seen it before, in the way Lukas and Jason looked at Cressida and Cecily, the way Anders looked at her.

"Caring about someone doesn't mean he can't be a fucking idiot," said Lukas. "He's already lost his memory. It's possible he could lose it again or undergo another drastic personality change. Dasha could be in danger."

Tears pricked at Valenna's eyes. She knew that, she just hated to think about it. "What do we do?" she asked.

Their response was in unison, so coordinated that for an instant, she wondered if they were sharing the same kind of broadcast link the Omega-Three-Omega cyborgs used: "Cecily."

"She'll be able to..." said Anders, just as Lukas said, "She knows..."

The cyborgs exchanged looks, and Anders continued first. "She'll know how to find the *Dragonfly*," he said. "And she knows how to get in and out of Zone space without drawing attention."

"I agree," said Lukas. "And while we've all taken care not to disturb Serena right now, she may be able to help, too."

Out of an abundance of caution given Serena's difficult pregnancy, all of them had done their best not to trouble their friend before her baby was born. But during their conversations, Valenna had the sense that Serena missed being included in regular activities and probably wasn't as delicate as everyone thought. She was past the nerve-wracking anxiety and fear that being the first known pregnant cyborg caused and the constant morning sickness. She was now mostly tired of being pregnant. Serena might very well welcome a distraction that wasn't baby-related.

"We'll have to go to the *Gray Ghost* anyway," said Valenna. "I'm sure she already sent a message to her dad, but we should see how he's doing."

She was dreading that talk. She knew how close Dasha and Dr. Caron were. This loss would devastate him.

"Let's do that now," said Lukas. "I'll send a note to Cressida, so she doesn't wonder where we've taken off to when she gets back, and we'll see if Cecily and Jason know, too." He dusted off his black-gloved hands. "Let's go."

Dasha lay down on the couch in the *Dragonfly*'s lounge, exhaustion pulling at her, a reminder that she hadn't slept well the night before.

Her physical needs overtaking her anger was *not* wanted at this time.

Remember the last time you slept? Yeah, and that stupid dream was even less appreciated right now. She could hardly remember it, just the feeling of his skin against hers, and...

She shook her head to chase away those thoughts.

Remember collapsing against him like the idiot damsel in distress you are? Even through his monk's robes, he'd been warm and solid, just the way she'd imagined him to be. Monks weren't supposed to have those kinds of bodies.

"God damn it," she whispered to herself, then threw her arm over her eyes in an attempt to block out some of the lounge's light. The entire ship was outfitted with illumination panels inset in the walls, a few centimeters from the decks. Adam and Esme's daughter, Rosie, was afraid of the dark.

Dasha couldn't help but smile at the memory of the little girl. Esme had explained that Rosie had never been afraid of the dark until she'd stepped aboard the *Dragonfly*, and the fear only seemed to crop up in space.

I'd better get back to Kurkay-2 in one piece so I can personally apologize to Adam and Esme for my role in this fiasco.

Rordan hadn't tried to make amends with her yet, which she appreciated because she wasn't ready to forgive him for this. She was fairly sure he hadn't snapped and wasn't about to do something to hurt her; her worries stemmed from what could happen after they crossed the border.

Dasha hadn't been to the Zone since she emigrated with her father when she was a child. And even when she'd lived there, her family resided on Cello Prime, one of the wealthier planets in a system known for its poverty. She didn't know the crushing grind of near-constant, precarious work, and she'd never lived in one of the Zone's hyper-polluted cities. She'd never known war. Everything facing her now was a giant, terrifying unknown, and if she died while there, it wouldn't be due to Rordan's missteps.

As if she'd summoned him with his thoughts, Rordan's footsteps sounded across the worn carpet stretching over the deck. "Dasha?"

His voice was soft, unsure. Dasha gritted her teeth, moved her arm, and sat up. "Yeah?"

"I promise I'll keep you safe."

She'd been hoping for an apology, an assurance that he'd changed course and turned the ship around, anything but that. "Fuck you."

The epithet left her before she could stop herself. But as she took in Rordan's surprised expression, she didn't feel sorry at all.

He didn't respond. He stood in front of the couch, motionless.

"I'm mad at both of us right now," she continued. "But mostly you. You could still turn around."

He shook his head. "We've come too far now."

"No, we haven't," she said. She got off the couch. She left the lounge and stalked down the corridor to the cockpit, Rordan trailing behind her. She didn't know why she hadn't thought to do this earlier. "We're going back to Kurkay-2."

She slid into the pilot's seat and stared at the tech array before her. She could fly a shuttle; wasn't a small passenger ship like the *Dragonfly* just a big shuttle? She could do this.

But a message glowed on the control panel, in big red letters: COMMAND LOCKED.

"What did you do?" she demanded, whirling around in the seat to face Rordan.

He blushed a little under the cockpit's sickly yellow lights. "I made some adjustments," he said.

"No shit. This is a civilian ship. What kind of adjustments?"

He tapped his head. "I can interface with it."

That was just fucking great. Dasha felt like screaming in frustration. "So, you're okay with being a cyborg now? What happened to a simple life of prayer?"

It was a low blow. If she was Rordan, she would hate herself right now.

"I'm using what I have to regain my life," he said, his voice sharper than she'd ever heard it. "If I can seamlessly integrate myself into this ship's technology, I will. This doesn't stop my being an adherent of the stars."

His eyes narrowed. "I'm not asking for sympathy from you. I know I don't deserve it right now. But I do need to know where I came from and how I came to be in this state. I don't need to have my entire memory back, but I do need to know why I went to Spaceport 44 after our rescue and what was done to me there. I may be able to get information about disreputable types who would hunt down someone like me. And I need you, but I don't know why."

Dasha's breath caught.

If he hadn't spirited her away, if he hadn't lost his memory, if he wasn't a monk, if they weren't running for their lives... so many impossibilities ran through her mind at his words.

"And then we're going right back to Kurkay-2," Rordan said. "It won't be more than a day."

Dasha wanted to believe him. He seemed to believe that they wouldn't be away from Bravan space that long. But there was no way a cyborg with a price on his head, deliberately headed to an unsecured public spaceport, would be allowed to just waltz into the Zone and leave without anyone noticing or caring.

"You know what?" she said. "We have to live with each other in a small space. Let's agree to get along until we get back to Kurkay-2." She took another look at the locked command console and tamped down her irritation. "You'd better get me back home in one piece."

His metallic eyes fixed on her, an unfamiliar intensity reflected in them. "I will."

What would Father Nelo think of him right now?

Rordan closed his eyes, not in prayer, but as a way to center himself as his brain and body synced to the *Dragonfly*'s systems as he stood in the cockpit's doorway, facing the corridor. His nanobots attuned themselves to the ship's systems, and he could feel the rush of the ship through space as she approached the Bravan-Zone border.

He was flying the ship with muscle memory, albeit one that had been greatly enhanced. He suspected that he would be able to fight with as much, too.

Had he been this cocky before he lost his memory?

He hoped not. Dasha's safety depended on it.

Maybe Father Nelo would be pleased about that, at least. He hadn't become totally selfish.

"And I am," he murmured to himself as the *Dragonfly* approached the border checkpoint. "I'm a completely selfish bastard for dragging her along."

He'd lied to her earlier about not knowing why he needed her with him.

I like her. I'm attracted to her. And I shouldn't be. For that reason alone, he likely wouldn't be fit to return to the Glissat temple.

He was jolted out of his thoughts when the ship's external comm alerted him to the border checkpoint, followed by an anxious moment as the ship's ident details were automatically verified before the *Dragonfly* was cleared to enter the Zone.

"They're probably wondering why someone would leave the Brava System in the first place," muttered Rordan to himself. "There's nothing here that makes it worth staying for."

But his attention wasn't focused on their impending arrival in the Zone. Instead, his nanobots had tuned him into what the other, precious passenger was doing: sitting at the small deck-locked table in the galley, nursing a cup of tea, and scowling.

His heart ached at the sight. She had every right to be angry with him.

Focus on your mission.

He'd heard that before. It wasn't from Garrett Jacoby, but a drill sergeant.

Another memory shard surfaced: standing at attention with a group of recruits, irritation and shame twanging through him. The other guys had been making fun of him for —what? He searched the remains of his memories.

He was rich, that was it. He was from Garshan. That set him apart from the other recruits.

His presence had caused a ruckus; he'd been targeted for harassment. And the distraction pissed off their instructor.

Focus on your mission. If you don't, you'll get yourself blown up.

There was something else that the instructor said, but Rordan couldn't remember the exact phrasing. Something about how commanding officers would look away if something happened to a soldier whose stupid actions caused a fatality.

He stopped searching his memories for the rest of that experience. *Just focus.*

The *Dragonfly* had made it past the border without arousing any suspicions. Next, she had to get to Spaceport 44, and he concentrated again, his integrated brain setting a ship's course. At least it was close to the border and they would be there within an hour.

The ships' sensors didn't pick up anything suspicious in the surrounding space lanes, and Rordan relaxed a little, then mentally explored the rest of the ship. He ached to stay focused on the galley, taking in the sight of Dasha from every angle, but forced himself to bypass her in favor of what the *Dragonfly* offered in the way of defenses.

And there wasn't much. The ship was equipped with an antiquated laser cannon and a weapons locker bereft of the heat signatures that indicated live charges.

He'd promised to keep Dasha safe, and he was taking her to Spaceport 44 unarmed.

Still, a lack of charge indicators didn't mean the ship was completely without weaponry. Rordan couldn't see how a cyborg as protective of his family as Adam must be would have a passenger ship without any hand weapons.

He made the short trip to the ship's weapons locker, located in a storage room directly beneath the cockpit. At least he didn't have to walk through the ship and see Dasha while he did so, he mused as he descended the stairs. His monk's robe billowed around him as he moved, reminding him of what he no longer was.

Not a soldier, not a monk. What am I, if I'm none of those things?

He opened the weapons locker and smiled. He didn't remember Adam Johnston, and from what he knew of Omega-Three-Omega, they hadn't worked together that long, but Rordan would hug the man if he could right now. Strapped against the locker's back wall was a pair of rifles, but not the energy weapons he'd worked with in the military. No, these used bullets: the rifles would require a better aim than that of their energy-based counterparts.

"That explains why I didn't pick up the signatures," he murmured, then picked up a weapon, hefting its weight. It was heavier than he expected, more solid. His muscle memory kicked in again, and he checked its chamber. Empty, of course. The responsible way to store weaponry when there was a small child in the family.

Either that, or there weren't any bullets to be found on the

Dragonfly. The locker had been left open, after all. Adam and Esme likely never had any need to use a weapon in the Brava System.

A quick check of the locker proved his hunch correct, and he didn't find any bullets. Rordan considered the rifle, then decided to bring it with him when they reached the spaceport anyway. If a potential assailant thought he was armed, he was likelier to be left alone.

"What are you doing?"

Rordan snapped to attention and whirled around to face the doorway where Dasha waited, disapproval written across her face. There was no point in trying to hide the rifle in his hands, and he gave her a sheepish look. "I'm checking the weapons," he said uselessly.

She raised an eyebrow. "A monk will get enough attention as is without that antique," Dasha replied.

There was a storage closet next to the weapons locker, and Rordan hoped it held some clothes that weren't monk's robes. He replaced the rifle where he found it, then opened the closet. "Thank the stars," he said when he saw it was full of fabric.

Dasha joined him, and he thought he could detect the faint scent of her shampoo over the musty smell in the storage room. "Anything good?"

Was that question friendly? He couldn't tell.

Rordan dug into the closet and pulled out a handful of men's clothes, all cheap ready-mades that might be as old as the *Dragonfly* herself. But they were intact and all in dark colors, which would help him stay as inconspicuous as possible while at the spaceport.

Barely lit in some areas... the smell of darfin and sweat in the recycled air...

The memory of the spaceport assaulted him and nearly dropped the faded olive drab shirt and trousers he'd been holding. His internal sensors told him that they were nearly at their destination, that he needed to get ready for whatever secrets the spaceport held for him.

"Rordan?"

Dasha's hand on his arm dragged him away from the memory and his growing unease. When he glanced at her, all he could see was concern.

Concern he didn't deserve.

"It's nothing," he said. "We're nearly there. I'm going to get changed, okay?"

He'd go to the captain's cabin; he knew Dasha would grant him some privacy there. Without another word, he draped a couple of garments over his arm and left the storage room.

As soon as he was alone, he slipped out of the voluminous robe and pulled on the new clothes. They fit fairly well, although he was a little disconcerted with the T-shirt leaving his arms exposed thanks to months of wearing his robe. He felt exposed in a way that he couldn't remember feeling before.

But it wasn't just physical. As angry as she was with him, Dasha had still managed to sneak past the defenses he hadn't known he had.

An alarm pinged in his head, and he froze, all thoughts about his exposed arms evaporating.

"Arrival at Spaceport 44 is imminent," the comp sensors intoned in his head. "Docking authorization has been approved. Proceed at your own risk."

Rordan caught a glimpse of himself in the mirror bolted to the wall. Reflected there was a man he hardly recognized: the close-cropped dark hair and glinting dark eyes were the same, but that was where the similarities ended. The faded green and gray clothes showed off his soldier's powerful build, something he never gave any thought to when he was still at the Glissat temple, and his scowl would be a warning to others to leave him alone.

There, his body was a vessel that helped him improve the lives of everyone on Glissat: planting food, building structures. Brother Rordan was a gentle and kind man.

But the man staring back at him looked like anything but.

And while he hoped he could return to being Brother Rordan of the Order of the Benevolent Stars, knowing what he might have to do at the spaceport, he doubted it.

CHAPTER 11

OF COURSE, Rordan would look good in his salvaged clothes. Dasha was struck speechless for the first few seconds he was in the lounge. She closed her eyes briefly, gathered herself, and then stood up, facing him squarely.

"I'm going with you," she announced.

"Are you sure that's wise?" Rordan hefted the antique rifle in his hands, his expression disdainful. He'd found a weapons bag in the same storage area and fitted it around the rifle to disguise it.

"No, but hopping on a stolen ship in an attempt to convince you to stay put on Kurkay-2 wasn't wise, either, but it's only the latest in a string of stupid decisions I've made recently." She ticked the items off her fingers. "I killed a guy to start off with, then I went exploring on his ship when I should've been helping more to get rid of the evidence. And I'm here because I thought I could talk you out of coming here."

"I wouldn't hold killing Janek Dalton against you," Rordan said. "He would have done far worse to you and your loved ones."

"Well, killing him meant I was on his ship and got stuck in the escape pod."

"Which you used to help me," Rordan said. "You potentially saved the entire order, the entire *population*, of Glissat because you did that. You're a hero."

Damn it, Dasha didn't want accolades right now. "I helped you cut out your ident chip when we should've waited until we saw my dad."

"Do I have to remind you of the escape pod's coordinates? Someone else could've easily obtained that information, who wasn't as inept as Dalton." He slung the holstered rifle over his shoulder. "Remember my previous comments about Glissat. I care deeply about the people there."

Dasha felt like stomping her foot in frustration. Why was he being so nice about everything she'd fucked up?

Before she could reply, he said, "Removing the chip was my idea. I was prepared to take the risk of injury or death. And I thought, at that point, that I would be willing to risk death if it meant I couldn't return to the temple." He paused, choosing his words. "I don't know if I can go back, and I don't want to die. I think that's an improvement."

This was news to Dasha. "Why can't you go back?"

"I don't know if I can be a monk in light of my memories returning," Rordan replied. "There are certain things about my past that I can't reconcile with a pious life. I need to find those memories so I can make an informed decision, both for my benefit and that of the temple." He sighed. "Are you ready to go?"

"You're not going to forbid me from leaving the ship?"

"I get the feeling that even if I did, you'd leave anyway," he said. "You're an adult. You can make these choices for yourself." He paused again. "I also don't trust a spaceport with an open docking policy to be especially secure. I don't think you'd be safe alone onboard the ship."

He'd given in easier than she expected. "Okay. Let's go."

Unease gripped Dasha as soon as they disembarked the *Dragonfly* and noticed the lack of people in the docking area. There was a single person in a plastiglas-walled booth in the dock's accessway that she assumed acted as the spaceport's version of transit control, although he didn't look up when she and Rordan left the dock. She shivered, and not just from the cold.

The accessway was just as cold as the docks and smelled like burned fuel and sweat. The odor only intensified when they walked to what she assumed was the spaceport's main concourse, where the lights were dim and only intermittently worked. The concourse was lined with storefronts, most of them closed, and the ones that were open didn't have signs indicating what was sold or services offered.

But Rordan seemed to know where he was headed, and Dasha walked briskly alongside him, trying to put aside her growing dread.

"How much for the girl?"

The voice rang out through the nearly empty concourse, and Dasha yelped. A man emerged from one of the unmarked storefronts, blocking their path and introducing the smell of spoiled food to Dasha's nostrils.

"Excuse me?" she said, voice higher than usual. Despite the bravado in her voice, she couldn't help but shrink back a little behind Rordan.

"Not for sale," Rordan said. He grabbed her arm and guided her around the man without saying another word or looking back.

"What the hell was that?" Dasha whispered.

"I don't know. Maybe he's looking for a good time, or..." Rordan's mouth set in a tight line. "Something else. Worse."

In a place like Spaceport 44, where even the military didn't bother with what on there, Dasha was willing to bet that the man's intentions fell into the "something else, worse" category. Another shiver overtook her body, one that had nothing to do with the cold.

And the concourse was almost as cold as the dock and airlock. She wrapped her sweater a little more tightly around herself.

"Are you cold?" Rordan asked.

"Yeah."

"If I had a coat, I'd give it to you."

Despite her fear over their situation, Dasha gave him a small smile. "Thank you. Aren't you cold?"

"No, I'm a cyborg," he whispered in her ear, his breath ruffling her hair.

Oh, right. He could modify his own body temperature, should he so choose. If they weren't on a notorious spaceport with no security, she would've remembered that.

Or maybe she wouldn't have. The feel of his breath tickling her hair, innocent as it was, sent a frisson of awareness through her body.

He was close enough to her that she thought she was picking up waves of his body heat, another distraction she couldn't afford right now. *Focus. We're in a very dangerous place.*

"Are you remembering anything?" she whispered.

"I know what direction we're supposed to be heading," he replied. "And it's unnerving. I feel like I'm about to find out something important." He unexpectedly reached for her hand and clasped it, the motion temporarily making her breath stutter. "I'm worried for you, but I'm glad you're with me right now."

Someone stepped out of a storefront and leered at them, his mouth full of cheap metallic teeth that shone in the dim light. Dasha shuddered and leaned closer to Rordan.

"I took you for selfish reasons," he said. He squeezed her hand.

Dasha was still conflicted about that: she was angry at both of them, for not having a conversation about taking off in their friend's ship on a whim. Her feelings for Rordan weren't entirely platonic, and she was starting to suspect, based on the way he still held her and the look he sent her way, that his feelings weren't, either.

And they'd voluntarily crossed the border to explore a spaceport known for its criminal activity. If they got out of this alive, they desperately needed to have that conversation.

They turned, following the concourse's path, until they reached a doorway, the door itself long gone. DOCTOR IS THAT WAY was crudely scrawled on the wall, with a couple of painted arrows to drive the point home. The dim illumination gave way to harsh yellow lights that glared at them from the ceiling every two or three meters. A single plastiglas window revealed the starry landscape outside.

I hate space travel. I hate the cold.

For half a second, she let herself think of her home on Sidra Prime, the nearby beach at Princess Cay, and wondered if Rordan would like it.

He noticed her turning away from the window. "Is something wrong?"

"Besides the obvious?" Without waiting for an answer, she said, "I hate space, is all. I'm not afraid of traveling, but I'm a planetside kind of person. Princess Cay is still my home."

"I'd keep Princess Cay to yourself," Rordan said quietly. "And maybe we should consider limiting our speech unless you can modify your accent to sound like you're from Echo-7 or one of the other inner worlds."

He had a point she hadn't considered before. An accent from one of the richest planets in the Brava System would attract attention.

Rordan squeezed her hand again, lending her a little reassurance.

The sharp whine of a laser weapon being discharged reminded her again of just how dangerous the spaceport was, and she jumped. She looked behind her but didn't see anyone, just heard the sound of the weapon again, followed by footsteps.

"What was that?" she asked uselessly, just as Rordan looked around the corridor for somewhere to hide.

"I'll fucking kill you!" someone roared in their direction.

Another, higher-pitched laser sounded, its report a sharp staccato against a wall. Rordan grabbed her and hauled her to the nearest doorway in an alcove off the corridor. But when he tried its handle, it wouldn't budge.

The footsteps were approaching faster now, as did the sounds of laser fire. "I think there are more than two people," Dasha said.

Rordan nodded, then pushed her against the door before sticking his head out of the alcove.

"That was mine!" another voice shouted. He accentuated his point with another blast from his weapon.

"Stars help us," said Rordan, ducking back into the alcove. His body blocked Dasha's in the small space, and she hoped that would be enough to protect both of them.

He was unarmed and without his memory. If whoever out there decided to pick on them, they were screwed.

Dasha silently said a quick prayer to the stars, banking that Rordan's faith in them would get them through this alive.

"Who's that?"

The voice sounded like it was directly behind Rordan and resembled the one who'd threatened to kill someone. Before she could collapse to the deck in fright, Rordan's arms wrapped around her waist, and he pulled her closer to him, then slanted his mouth over hers.

Dasha froze, the shock of it making her forget her terror. A second later, she responded, arms circling his neck and kissing him back.

But he lurched into her, breaking their kiss, and both of them looked up to see the metallic-toothed man from the concourse, the barrel of his laser rifle against Rordan's ribs.

"Do you mind?" Rordan snarled. He rose to his full height, considerably taller than his assailant. "This isn't a good time."

"Never a good time. Who the fuck are you?"

"No one you need to worry about. Go find your friend and shoot him."

He squinted at Rordan. "I've seen you before."

"I doubt that. Now, fuck off."

Dasha barely contained a squeak of surprise. She'd never heard Rordan use that kind of language or that tone of voice. In that instant, she finally saw what kind of soldier he must have been, what kind of cyborg. He was powerful, but he'd hidden that away as a novice monk.

The metallic-toothed man backed away half a meter but didn't lower his weapon. "Your fuckin' soldier friends are on the way. If you get caught here, they'll kill you. They don't like their kind at this spaceport."

"I'm not a soldier. Now kindly *fuck off*."

Further down the corridor, someone shouted, "Got him!" There was another screech of lasers scoring metal, then someone yelped.

The man took off without another word at them, and Dasha said a quick prayer of thanks to the stars. Aloud, she said, "Thank you, Rordan."

There was a hungry look on his face when his eyes met

hers. A different kind of shiver than the ones she'd been having since disembarking the *Dragonfly* rippled through her. She knew that look. She'd never expected to see it from him.

"I'm sorry," he said.

"Don't be," she said. "Not for that."

"I've taken enough from you already."

"It gave us cover," she replied. "I've never been saved by a kiss before, but there's a first time for everything."

He visibly relaxed a little, but the longing look he sent her way didn't abate. On impulse, Dasha raised herself on her toes to meet his face and pressed a light kiss to his lips.

His dark gaze searched her face, surprised.

"This is really complicated," she said. "But I want us to get out of this alive, and then we'll talk about the complications, okay?"

He nodded, then opened his mouth to speak.

But he was cut off when an alarm tore through the spaceport. "Military en route," a bored voice intoned. "This is a warning."

"We have to go," yelled Rordan over the noise. He grabbed her hand, and they ran down the corridor.

***

They had to get to the makeshift lab where he'd had his surgery. For some reason, Rordan had the sense that place was safe, or as safe as one could be on Spaceport 44.

The brawling people who'd been firing off lasers were long gone, probably to hideouts Rordan wouldn't be privy to, which provided a small measure of relief. He could only deal with one problem at a time right now.

Speaking of problems... he looked at Dasha, who was starting to lag in their haste. He stopped, and in a quick, smooth motion, picked her up and draped her over his shoulder.

"What the hell?" Dasha said into his back. She wiggled a little against him, and it took a few seconds for him to realize that she was readjusting the rifle strapped to his back.

"It's just easier this way." The motion also provided him the benefit of holding her in addition to being faster, so it wasn't cause for complaint.

The corridor branched off, and he racked his brain, trying to remember which way he'd taken the last time he was here. *Right. I went right. Of course, it's the corridor with all the lights burned out.*

And that darkness wasn't a cover due to the incoming military raid, either. It was just a creepy, dim corridor.

His night vision activated as he ran for the lab he knew was close to the end of the corridor. The siren wasn't quite so loud here, and his cybernetics had dulled the noise somewhat, but it still clanged through his head. He could only imagine how uncomfortable it was for Dasha.

Harsh yellow light spilled from a cracked and filthy plastiglas door at the end of the corridor. Rordan halted about three meters from the doorway, then helped Dasha down. Even disheveled, eyes wild, she was still beautiful, and he hoped he had the chance to kiss her again.

More than kiss her. What had happened in that doorway reminded him of something that had been dormant for a long time, forgotten until today. He didn't think he could go back to being a monk.

He shook his head, trying to clear away that thought. This was the worst possible time to be thinking about what remained of his faith.

"Is this it?" Dasha asked. She peered in the darkness at something on the wall. "What does that say? It's too dark to make out."

Rordan honed in on it. He didn't remember seeing it the last time he was here, but that wasn't saying much.

Someone had painstakingly carved a message into the wall, and it looked like the words were cut with a knife.

Or a metal scalpel.

"'Refuge,'" Rordan said. He touched the word. "'Services for the downtrodden.'"

Dasha looked at the doorway and shuddered. "Is this it?"

"Yeah." He took her hand again and hoped he wasn't about to make a terrible mistake. "Let's look inside."

Dr. Caron was so still that if he hadn't blinked, Cressida thought he might have found a way to turn himself into a statue.

Maybe he'd already made such a discovery. God knew he was brilliant enough for it.

She exchanged a quick glance with Lukas, who made the tiniest shrug of his shoulders in response.

"Dr. Caron?" Cressida said, not for the first time. "Is there anything we can do to make this easier right now?"

Her query was met with silence. She looked at everyone else assembled in her sister's kitchen—Valenna herself, Anders, Lukas, Cecily and Jason, Adam, Matthias, and Serena—but no one was forthcoming with a solution.

Poor Serena. The younger woman sat in a chair next to Dr. Caron, hand on her very pregnant belly. If she hadn't known better, Cressida would've thought Serena was carrying twins.

Dr. Caron took his first audible breath since he sat down at the table. Before anyone could react, he slammed his fist on the tabletop.

"That bastard!" he roared. "He took my daughter!"

Half a second later, everyone started to speak at once.

"She said in her message that she's fine," said Valenna.

"He wasn't a sadist or anything like that on Omega-Three-Omega," said Jason. "He isn't a bad guy."

"Dasha said he promised that she and my ship would be returned in one piece," said Adam. At Dr. Caron's murderous look, Adam quickly added, "Of course, Dasha's the priority. I don't think Rordan is on a suicide mission."

"But he's going to Spaceport 44," said Cecily. "That's not exactly the safest place in the Zone to be under any circumstances." That remark drew daggers from everyone else at the table, the worst from Dr. Caron. Cecily held up her hands. "I'm not going to sugarcoat it. That place exists so the galaxy's flotsam has somewhere to hang out in one place. But Rordan's a cyborg and a monk. This adventure he's taken Dasha on, they'll come back."

"I don't know if he's had a psychotic break," Dr. Caron snapped. Cressida cringed at the tone in his voice, warranted as it was. He was ordinarily a calm, collected beacon all of them needed and cherished. His being so off-balance, while justified, sent shockwaves through everyone crammed in the kitchen.

"I don't like to refer to any of you as 'models,'" Dr. Caron continued. His voice was low, tight with anger and grief. "You know I think it erases your humanity and reduces you down to bags of bolts. But for want of a better term, Rordan is the most advanced model out of all of you. Garrett Jacoby expanded on my original research in ways I never dreamed possible, let alone ethical, and there's certainly a possibility that Rordan experienced some kind of break I couldn't have anticipated."

"We can get her back," said Jason. "Cecily and I are certainly capable of infiltrating Spaceport 44."

"I've been there before," Cecily chimed in. "Twice, in my early days in my old... career." She shot a quick glance at Anders, but his expression didn't change. He hadn't cared for

Cecily's work as a mercenary and assassin for hire. "It's a shitheap," she added. "Sorry."

"Is there anything in Rordan's blueprints and medical information that might tell you about his mental state?" Cressida asked.

"No," Dr. Caron replied. "There's nothing that would indicate his amnesia, either. I'm dealing with a lot more variables and unknowns than I did with the rest of you."

"We'll go and bring them back," Jason said. He looked at Cecily, who nodded in agreement. "We're forces to be reckoned with on our own."

"I'll go, too," said Adam.

"If anything happens to you, Esme will kill you," said Cecily. "I know I would."

"You've already killed people for me," said Jason.

"I know. And I'd do it again."

As much as Cressida liked Cecily, hearing her talk about killing people, whether or not they deserved it, made her queasy. *Dasha killed someone, too.*

Was that one of the reasons she'd agreed to go with Rordan? Grief, shame? A desire to get away from the place where she did it, even though it was in self-defense?

"It's so rare to hear a sentiment that's sweet *and* fucked up," said Anders. "But seriously. Dr. Caron, any of us would go to bring back Dasha and Rordan, so you can kick his ass."

Dr. Caron glowered. "Thank you."

To Matthias, Lukas said, "We understand if you want to sit this one out."

Matthias affectionately squeezed Serena's shoulder. "I appreciate that."

"There's just one thing," said Serena, finally piping up. "Would you be taking the *Gray Ghost*?"

"Yeah," said Cecily cautiously. "Why?"

"It's the sickbay," Serena said. She winced and shifted in

her seat. "It's not like I can go to the hospital in Westingtown. I, uh..."

The knot of anxiety Cressida had been carrying since she heard about Dasha and Rordan taking off grew. *Does she mean...?*

"I think my water broke," said Serena. She smiled as Matthias paled. "I'm going into labor."

CHAPTER 12

RORDAN KEPT one arm wrapped around Dasha, and with his free hand, he pounded on the dirty plastiglas door. *What the fuck kind of nickname is 'Refuge'? And why am I swearing? Did it come easily to me before I lost my memory?*

He could hardly focus on anything besides Dasha's warm, trembling weight against him and the unending klaxon that heralded the military's arrival. *Are they after me, or is it some kind of routine raid?* He knocked again. If it didn't open, he would break it down.

The door finally eased open a couple of centimeters. "Piss off," said a garrulous voice from behind the plastiglas. "Fuckin' red alert going on right now, bud. Not a good time."

"Let me in," commanded Rordan, his tone surprising even himself. "We've met before. I need some answers from you."

The door opened a little further, and a wizened, white-haired old man peered out. "Stars and universe around us," he yelled over the noise. "It's *you*."

"So, you know me?"

"Sure fuckin' do, Captain. Are you here to kill me? I'm armed back here."

"I'm not going to kill you, but you have to let us in," said Rordan.

The old man looked at Dasha, who gave him a little wave and a small, tight smile. "Fuck," he said. He heaved a gusty sigh. "I know you won't leave of your own free will. Come in."

Rordan and Dasha gratefully slipped past the door. "I'm armed, be warned," the old man said again. He sealed the door behind them, blocking out much of the siren's noise. "Now, what are you here for this time?" He reached for Rordan's arm. Before he could react, the old man looked at the exposed ports. "Guess the syntho-skin fell off, just like I told you it would." He let Rordan's arm drop.

"It's my memory," Rordan blurted. "Not the syntho-skin."

"Well, the ports aren't that bad, anyway. And I told you last time, wear long sleeves."

Long sleeves? Rordan remembered the voice of the man who doled out that advice. Now he could put a face to it.

The old man inclined his head at Dasha. "Who's this?"

"I'm here about the procedures I had the last time I visited," Rordan said, ignoring the question. "My memory's gone. Some things are coming back to me, but until a few days ago, I didn't know who I was, just that my name was Rordan."

The old man shrugged. "That's all you need when you're a monk. Your first name."

Rordan felt like shaking him if it meant he could get answers. "What happened when I came here Who are you?"

The old man ticked off his answers on his fingers. "You asked me to reset your memory, my name is Theodore Best but call me Ted, you came here because you knew about my black market surgery outfit here, and I did exactly as you asked. I reset you, patched you up to make you as human-looking as possible, and put you on the first civilian passenger shuttle to Glissat. I knew you'd be safe with a bunch of monks, at least for a while."

"Best," Dasha whispered.

"Do you know him?" Rordan asked.

"No," she replied. "But—Mr. Best. Are you acquainted with Lukas Best?"

The old man—Ted—swallowed, and the color drained from his face. "Shit. Is he after me, too?"

It hadn't escaped Rordan's mind that someone from Kurkay-2 might have taken it upon themselves to stage a rescue mission, and Lukas, the original cyborg, might be among the cavalry. That made it all the more important to find out what happened to him at Spaceport 44, see if it could be reversed, and get away from the Zone as soon as possible.

"No," said Dasha, answering Ted's question for Rordan. "Not that we know of."

"And who are you?" the old man asked.

She hesitated for a second before speaking. "Dasha Caron."

Rordan didn't think it was possible for Ted to look any more unwell, but he was proven wrong. "You're Marshall Caron's daughter."

Dasha seemed unsurprised at his conclusion. "Yeah. I'm sure if you know Lukas Best, you'd know my father."

Ted double-checked the locks on the plastiglas door, then pressed a biometric lockpad next to the doorway. A grinding sound filled the air, mingling with the klaxon, as a secured safety door descended over the plastiglas one.

"If either of you wanted to kill me, you'd have done it by now," Ted announced. He shuffled back to them, pressing his hand on his lower back as he did so. "That door will buy us some time from the military if we need it."

Impatience flooded Rordan at the man's dithering. "I have some questions for you," he said, voice even. "I need answers."

"I'm sure you do. Follow me."

Dasha shot him a sympathetic look as they walked behind Ted. The foyer they'd been standing in gave way to a narrow hallway, its metallic walls pitted, to a harshly lit makeshift lab. A surgical table was in the middle of the room, one of its legs replaced with a length of pipe, and a single, darkened screen was affixed to the wall.

Rordan froze. *I've been here before.*

He'd walked through that concourse, ignoring everyone he passed by who made rude remarks or offered him darfin, straight for this lab.

How did I know to contact this man? Who is he?

"I can see some wheels are turning in your head," said Ted, a smug undercurrent to his voice. "Just enough so you know you've been here before, but not much else. Am I right?"

"How did I know to come here?"

"Why don't you start by telling me what you remember?" Ted suggested.

It would have been an innocent idea, had Rordan not approached this man for an illegal, black market surgery.

He quickly looked at Dasha, but her face had the same suspicious expression that he was sure mirrored his own. *What I wouldn't give for us to have the kind of mental link I had on Omega-Three-Omega with the others. Or on the* Dragonfly.

It was too dangerous to attempt that kind of maneuver here, even without the military's impending arrival. What good was being a cyborg if he couldn't even use his cybernetics?

"No," Rordan replied. "I'd rather you tell me what you know about my past and why I came here." He looked around the lab. "And why I knew to visit you."

He'd been left here even though Cecily had tried to talk

him out of it, to just let her take him to the Brava System with the rest of the surviving cyborgs.

Ted fussed with a stool, heaving himself on it with a dramatic sigh. "All right," he said. "You're from Garshan."

"I know that much."

Dasha's hand curled around his, and he accepted the gesture, grateful for her nearness.

"So am I. The admiral's my cousin. You remember Stephen Best? Lukas's father?"

Rordan shook his head.

"Just as well. You and Lukas weren't playmates, anyway, although I was your neighbor for quite a few years when you still lived at home. Lukas wasn't allowed to have friends. He was born so he could be a cyborg, you know. Supposed to show off the might of the Zone's military." To Dasha, he said, "Your father was in charge of that program in its early days."

"He refined cybernetic technology," she said. "It wasn't meant to turn into what it did." Her mouth set in a thin line. "What the military did to Lukas and Rordan was inhumane and monstrous."

"Lukas wasn't my kid, so that was none of my business," Ted retorted. "I don't get involved in others' affairs."

"Even though Lukas was abused?" Dasha said. "He's told me as much."

"What do you care?"

"I'm a teacher," Dasha shot back. "I care about children's welfare very much."

"Not my point," Ted replied. "You're all from Garshan. Rich planet, rich families. Including yours, Rordan, although you told me last time you were here that they're all gone now, and they disapproved of your career when you enlisted. You were first in your graduating class at your university. Supposed to be a professor, you said, but you never got past your undergrad thanks to the war. Still, that's a hell of a lot more time in school than the rest of the sad sacks existing in the Zone.

"Both you and Lukas ending up cyborgs was just God playing a shitty joke on you two," he continued. "You showed up here, demanded I erase your memory of everything that made you a cyborg, and that was that." He held out his hands. "I did that, put you on that ship to the Glissat temple, and that was supposed to be the end of it."

Rordan considered Ted's words, knew there was plenty the old man wasn't telling him. "How would I know to come to you?" he asked.

"I worked on the early cyborg project," Ted replied. Dasha gasped. "Not as a doctor or in research and development. I was a military nurse until I was discharged and then set up shop here. I'm the go-to for the poor people who need a wound cauterized or scar camouflaged. Although I'm sure you've noticed by now that my syntho-skin supplies aren't that great."

"You still didn't answer my question."

Ted shrugged. "You said you found me on the galactic net. You'd heard about an ex-nurse who would do anything for money and not talk about it, figured I might have the tools for makeshift brain surgery, and you were right. I work under my own name, and you would've recognized that from when we lived next door to each other. No big mystery there."

"Can you undo it?"

Dasha elbowed him a little. He didn't have to speak to know she was asking if he'd lost what was left of his mind.

"I don't like meddling in cybernetic brains," Ted said. "So, no. I'm not fixing that for you. If some of your memories are coming back on their own, they'll probably all come back at some point."

"That doesn't make sense!" Rordan exploded. "If you

don't like cybernetic brains, why did you operate on me in the first place?"

"You transferred me half a million scrip," Ted said, his voice rising. "Half a fucking million scrip for illegal brain surgery, and you paid in full upfront. If something had gone wrong, I would've shunted you out the nearest airlock, and no one would've fucking cared because you chose to have medical treatment from an ex-nurse working out of Spaceport 44. Do you get it?" He leaned a little closer, wobbling on the edge of his stool. "I had nothing to lose."

Stars and universe, I am a stupid, naive man.

It would explain why he'd let himself get talked into undergoing cybernetic enhancement, why he'd sought out black market surgery.

"So, you see why I'm not going to tinker with your head again?" Ted asked. "If for nothing else because someone's going to come looking for her." He nodded his head at Dasha. "She's loved and wanted, I'm sure. Although I'm sure that's not the reason the military showed up."

"Why are they here?"

Ted shrugged. "Once in a while, they like to pretend they're doing something about the scourge of Spaceport 44. The Zone's interior secretary was caught with a couple of sex workers and a stack of darfin patches a couple of days ago, so they need to deflect. The war's over, for now, so the spaceport's what they're focused on."

"You don't seem concerned."

"I'm not. But on the off-chance they're here for you two, I can't take any risks."

Ted moved far faster than Rordan expected of a man his age. Before he or Dasha could react, Ted removed a stunner from his back pocket and fired at each of them.

Dasha crumpled to the dirty deck first. Rordan remained frozen in place from the blast, and Ted fired again.

This time, it worked. Rordan crashed, hitting his head on the operating table and dislodging the pipe holding up one end. As the bed fell on him, hitting his back, Ted groused, "No one's taking my fucking money."

Then, like a switch being flipped, everything went dark.

"You're absolutely sure about this?" Ted crossed his arms over his chest. "You know all I can do to your circuits is tweak the settings, right?"

Circuits, settings... Rordan never wanted to hear those words again, along with myriad others that related to technology. "I said yes," he snapped. "I need to get this shit out of my head and go to the first place outside of the Zone where the tech doesn't exist and forget who I ever was. You wouldn't happen to know where I could do that?"

Valenna Merchant, the strange, frail girl with long, dark curly hair who'd been lured to Omega-Three-Omega came to mind. She and Anders Barris, that poor bastard stuck in a giant water tank for four years, had a batshit-crazy idea to start a homestead on one of the planets Zone refugees and ex-pats were flocking to. She'd offered Rordan a place to stay when they found a suitable property, along with the rest of the surviving cyborgs, but only Jason Formosa had accepted.

Rordan didn't farm. He didn't manhandle unruly livestock. All he knew was academia and the military. The former was an impractical career in the Zone, a place that constantly devalued and discouraged education, and he'd bungled the latter beyond his worst nightmares.

"I have nothing left," Rordan added. "No family, no friends."

"You were a whiny little bitch when you were a boy, too," Ted groused. "Your father would be disappointed in you."

Rordan resisted the urge to clock his former neighbor in the face, at least point out that Ted was dishonorably discharged from the military. But he didn't. "You wanted half a million," he said. "You'll get it. Can you do everything I asked?"

"Erase your memory and put you on the first ship to nowhere?" Ted gave Rordan a look that clearly questioned his intelligence. "Yeah. Pay up."

***

Rordan coughed, then rolled over on his back. As he did so, his hand brushed a warm body, whose breathing was shallower than he would have liked, but steady.

"Who turned off the lights?" he muttered and coughed again. The air tasted dirty, like the life support of whatever ship or station he was on had cycled off and on again. That would account for his being passed out on the floor.

Except it didn't. The memory of being hit with a stunner came back to him, and with it, remembering that Dasha was targeted, too.

His eyes adjusted to night vision, and he could make out Dasha next to him. He shook her shoulder. "Dasha." His voice was urgent.

She didn't need much encouragement to wake up, praise the stars. She turned on her side, blinking. "Rordan?" She coughed, and he helped her sit up. "All I can see is your eyes. What happened to Ted?"

Rordan scanned the empty lab. "The bastard ran off."

She coughed again, but he thought he detected a laugh in there, too. "That's the second time I've heard you swear."

"Are you all right?"

"Yeah." She tried to stand up, stumbled, and Rordan rose to his feet to help her. "Your eyes wouldn't happen to have flashlight abilities, would they?"

"No. But I can see enough to know that Ted's gone."

"What about life signs?" she asked, not letting go of his hand. He liked the feeling but tried not to be distracted by it. "I think Lukas can pick them up. Can you?"

"Not that I know of." Rordan concentrated, but his cybernetics didn't sense anything except the poor quality of the recycled air and the spaceport's cool temperature. "I guess I wasn't built with that feature."

"You know I don't think of you as a thing, don't you?"

"I was trying to make a joke."

"Oh." Dasha made small, cautious steps, and Rordan moved at her pace.

"I think I used to have a sense of humor, but it was subtle." He looked around the lab as if he would find a clue where Ted went, but there was nothing to indicate as such.

Dasha gripped his arm. "Did your memories come back after we were zapped?"

"I remembered coming here the first time," Rordan replied. "But I'd rather figure out what's going on and how to safely get off this spaceport before I start thinking about my memories."

"I understand. At least the siren's stopped."

She was right. In all of Rordan's confusion and worry, he hadn't noticed the silence. Did that mean the military was gone?

For the first time, he wished he had greater cybernetic abilities. What he wouldn't give to pick up life signs, or establish a link with the spaceport's computers. Unlike the free-for-all docking policy, he could sense that the rest of Spaceport 44's computer systems were much more secure.

They were at the lab's entrance now, the door still closed and locked. Breaking it down wouldn't be a problem for him; the issue was what was on the other side of the door. "I really wish I had life form sensors right now," he muttered.

"Maybe there's a vent or tunnel we could try instead," Dasha suggested.

It wasn't a great idea, but Rordan was realizing it was the only one they had for now. All spaceports and stations had maintenance tunnels large enough to accommodate an adult or two. "I'm sure there is," Rordan said. "There are probably a lot of hidey-holes in the tunnels and vents, and I don't want us to run into anyone who might've taken advantage of them." He sighed. "It would be really nice if more of my military training would come back to me right about now."

"Did you make another joke?"

"It wasn't so much a joke as making an astute observation based on a wish."

"You really know how to take the fun out of things," Dasha said. "It must've been the monks."

"No, it was my family, too." As he said the words, Rordan realized that he could plumb those depths of his memory, that clear pieces of his childhood recollections were returning. His stern parents. His childhood house on Garshan: large, airy, and sparsely decorated because his parents hated clutter. As a boy, his footsteps echoed wherever he walked.

There must have been something in his voice that gave him away, because Dasha whispered, "You sound different. Besides the obvious, are you okay?"

He was a soldier who'd forgotten his training. He was unarmed on a dangerous spaceport, with a price on his head, and he'd selfishly taken a precious woman with him when he took off to find out who he really was and what happened to him.

I'm not okay.

It took him a couple of seconds to answer, and he doubted she would believe him. "I don't know."

CHAPTER 13

SERENA COULDN'T HAVE SUMMONED the energy to sit up on her own even if she wanted to. Lying down right now was the most comfortable position she'd ever been in. *Thank you, Cecily, or whoever owned the* Gray Ghost *first, for springing for voice commands on all the medical equipment.* "Computer, raise the head of the diag bed ten centimeters." Her voice was more tired than she'd ever heard it before, but she didn't care. Instinctively, she placed a protective hand around the back of baby Sullivan's head. Still laying against her chest, sleeping, Sullivan didn't fuss at all. *I'm sure that won't last long.*

"You're smiling," Matthias said. "I haven't seen that from you in a long time."

"It's over," Serena replied. Despite her exhaustion, relief coursed through her. "I did it. I can't believe Dr. Caron said my labor was easy."

"Is there anything I can say about your labor that won't result in me being in the doghouse?"

She felt another smile bloom across her face. "Of course, always."

"It was three hours from start to finish, even though I

know it probably felt like it took a lot longer. Did my mother ever tell you what *my* arrival was like?"

Grace, Matthias's mother, had recently joined them in the Brava System, and the three of them—now four—were living in a rented house outside Westingtown. "She's going to love being a grandmother," Serena said. "And the name we picked." Sullivan was named for Matthias's late father.

"Yes, she told me. She let it slip that it took, and I quote, 'thirteen and a half hours of unremitting hell to birth you.'" She stroked Sullivan's back, the rise and fall of his tiny body as he breathed a reassurance.

Despite her happiness and relief, tears sprang to her eyes. "He's all right," she said, a sob catching in her throat. "Our baby's perfectly healthy."

"And you're perfectly healthy, too," said Matthias. She thought she could detect a lump in his catch in his voice, and she remembered the tension over much of the last year, their sheer terror at finding out she was pregnant. Then later, nervous hope for her future: dreams of family and motherhood that she'd never dared to voice when she was trapped on a moon compound. While Serena's nanobots were deactivated, no one knew how a cybernetically enhanced body would handle a pregnancy.

Being the only female cyborg in the galaxy only served to add another layer of worry and loneliness to her pregnancy. She suspected that her labor was shorter due to her cyborg status but couldn't be sure. Dr. Caron had already asked if she would be willing to have what remained of her nanobots examined in the coming days, something she was happy to do.

"I didn't know what to expect," Serena said as she let her tears fall. "I kept worrying that my nanobots would reactivate at random and something would go wrong, and I already wanted to be a mother by the time we found out, and I didn't think I could handle it if..." She kissed the top of Sullivan's head, trying to put her old fears to bed. Their son was healthy and whole, a 'bruiser,' as Dr. Caron put it, at four and a half kilograms at birth. "I know it was a shock to both of us, but I'm really happy to be a mom, you know? I never thought this would happen."

Sullivan was perfect, and she had to believe Dr. Caron's reassurances that her labor was, in fact, easy. Although if she compared it to her months-long battle with hyperemesis gravidarum and anxiety, it might very well be. "I think Dr. Caron was glad for the distraction," she said, then added, "I hope Dasha's okay."

She was a parent now. The idea of her son being whisked away had her tightening her hold on him a little more.

Matthias pressed a kiss to her lips. "I'm worried for Dasha and Rordan, too, but you have enough on your plate right now. Just focus on Sullivan." He beamed. "Holy shit, Serena. You delivered him like a pro. I'm proud of you."

Sullivan stirred. A small whimper escaped him, but he didn't fully wake up.

"I love you both so much," he said. He brushed back a wisp of Sullivan's dark hair, a feature that could have come from him or Serena. One thing that definitely came from Matthias, Serena thought, was his nose.

"I love you, too," she whispered. She kissed Sullivan's head, which was his cue to wake up and let out a cry.

"I think he's hungry. Computer, raise the bed another ten centimeters," said Serena. The bed obliged. With her free hand, she unlaced the top of her hospital gown. To Matthias, she said, "I think we've got this."

Rordan let go of Dasha's hand. "Stay put," he said. "We're at the door. I'm going to have to break it down."

She nodded, knowing he could see it, and hoped they weren't about to face a military squadron or someone from Wilton Intergalactic Fluid Technology. And they had to leave the lab; after Rordan thoroughly inspected the space, he couldn't find a weapon or a secret exit.

The water company! Was it possible they were behind the military raid? Dasha didn't remember much about living in the Zone, but she'd read about and heard enough from her father about the grip private corporations had on the entire region. It wasn't out of the question for a water company to pay off the military to bring back a cyborg for experimentation purposes.

Rordan interrupted her thoughts with a couple of well-placed kicks against metal and plastiglas. "Almost there," he muttered, before delivering another, final kick. Faint yellow light beckoned from the corridor, outlining Rordan like some kind of dark angel. His eyes still glowed, and they quickly scanned the area outside the lab. "It's empty," he whispered. "We're going to get back to the *Dragonfly*, I promise."

Dasha nodded. "I believe you."

He fixed his gaze on her, and she could feel its intensity even in the darkness. The look sent a frisson of heat running through her, a wholly inappropriate feeling at the moment. "I'm sorry," he said. "This was stupid, and I shouldn't have brought you here."

"But you found out why you came here in the first place," Dasha said. "You found out how you ended up on Glissat. It wasn't a waste of a trip."

"And I probably would've had my memory back in the coming months, anyway," Rordan replied. "Instead, I've needlessly put you in danger."

"I already told you that I volunteered to come with you," Dasha said. "And you know what? Why don't we just agree that we're both idiots, for different reasons, and move on?

Standing here, on a locked-down spaceport, arguing for the sake of arguing, won't save us."

He blinked, the motion all the more distinctive in the dark. "I'm not arguing. I'm apologizing."

"Okay, we're not arguing about arguing. But we should probably get moving, find a maintenance tunnel or something like you said before."

"I care about you," Rordan said. "More than I have for anyone in my life."

Dasha's breath hitched. "We haven't known each other that long."

"I remember my parents," he said. "I remember the house I grew up in and pieces of my life on Garshan, about the military. I never cared for anyone like I do you. And I'll do everything I can to keep you safe and bring you back home."

Dasha flashed back to The Sanctuary, the nickname her father gave the treehouse in Princess Cay she'd called home for most of her life. Then another image took shape: she and Rordan, enjoying a day at the beach. Basking in the sunlight, each with a beer in hand, and not a single rain cloud on the horizon.

As much as she liked her new friends on Kurkay-2, Sidra Prime was her home.

As crazy as it sounded to be the more important person in Rordan's life up to that point, she cared about him, too. Far more than she expected to after knowing him for such a short period of time.

"I'm going to hold you to that," she said. Impulsively, she reached for his face and kissed him.

His response was immediate. His arms tightened around her, bringing her closer to him and eliciting a gasp of surprise from her and setting every nerve ending in her body to high alert. But he pulled away before either of them could lose themselves, leaving her weak-kneed.

"What was that for?" he asked. She thought she could detect a smile in his voice.

"For good luck."

"Best good luck charm ever." He took her hand and urged her forward. "Let's go."

Fear had her on edge, and she stayed as close to Rordan as she could without him actually picking her up. They moved slowly, with Rordan examining walls for telltale seams that indicated hidden doorways, but nothing jumped out at him. Nor did any of the spaceport's residents, although Dasha figured that would change once they got to the main concourse.

If they got the concourse. Hopefully, they would find an alternate route to the docks before then.

"Sorry," she whispered. "I don't mean to keep clinging to you like a vine."

"I can work with that," he said. "Don't worry about it."

They turned, and he led her into the same alcove they'd hidden in when the fight broke out earlier, the one with the locked door. "Stand back a little," he whispered. "I'm going to find out what's behind it."

"Are you sure? It's probably a criminal clubhouse or something."

Rordan didn't reply, only moved back half a meter to give himself enough space to kick down the door.

"Damn it," she said softly and looked up as if to ask the stars for guidance.

In that instant, the emergency lighting switched itself off, and regular illumination resumed. There was a growl under their feet as if the spaceport was waking itself up, making Dasha jump.

She looked in either direction but didn't see anyone. Rordan, leg poised to deliver a vicious kick, looked a little confused as well.

Dasha waited for an announcement, but none came. Instead, the sound of dozens of pairs of booted feet stomping on the deck greeted her ears.

"Oh, shit," she said.

Rordan paled under the harsh yellow light. "I think that's the military," he said. They couldn't go back to the lab. It didn't have a place to hide, nor an escape. There was no way to return to the concourse without running into the soldiers.

She looked at the door. Rordan nodded, then kicked it again.

It gave way more easily than she expected, opening about half a meter with a rusty squeal. Rordan stuck his head inside, then gestured for Dasha to follow.

They stepped on a catwalk, and Rordan closed the door behind him as best he could. Ceiling lights revealed a jumble of rusted-out machinery resting on the floor below the catwalk, including pieces of what looked like an energy core.

The room was mercifully devoid of people, but they moved quickly along the catwalk. "We should be just passing the entrance to the concourse now," he murmured after a few moments of silence.

I'm glad he *thought to retrace our steps.*

They passed through a doorway that led to another empty maintenance room, although the equipment here looked newer. Some of it still hummed, a couple of pipes overhead delivering recycled air or whatever to the rest of the spaceport. But the sight made Dasha nervous; that could mean they were getting closer to a maintenance area that was still in wide use.

Finally, Rordan stopped in front of a ladder that stretched from the catwalk to the ceiling. "By my calculations, we're just past the concourse's main entrance," he said. "I spotted a door near here that might lead to it, but I don't want to chance it yet. I'm going to take a look up there, see if there's an access tunnel, and we'll find a way to the docks."

"I'm going with you."

He didn't argue. "At least let me go first."

Rordan climbed up the first rungs, and Dasha followed suit. "Is it bad that I don't mind being behind you?" she asked.

He looked over his shoulder. "What?"

Embarrassment twinged through her. "I'm trying to compliment your ass."

Color tinged his face as he understood. "Oh! Well, thank you."

Well, Dasha, what did you think flirting with a monk who's in battle mode would get you right now?

She answered her own question. *Nowhere.* At this point, she didn't know who was more out of practice.

The ladder led to a small, square platform that branched off into more catwalks. Rordan paused, considering where they were in relation to the spaceport's public areas, then picked a direction. The recycled air was growing colder here, a sure sign that they were closer to the docks.

Both of them looked down at the same time, and Dasha bit back a cry of surprise and fright.

A grate under the catwalk, rusted through in places, revealed the main concourse's entrance. Directly beneath them were a pair of black-uniformed Zone soldiers, and a trembling gray head Dasha recognized as Ted Best. A small duffel was slung over one shoulder.

"I told you, I don't know," Ted was saying. Even though they had to be three meters above the small group, Dasha could hear the desperation in the old man's voice. "He came here nearly a year ago for surgery, I did the surgery like he asked, and he fucked off. He came here again right before you guys swooped in. I don't know where he is now."

"We have confirmation that someone broke out of your illegal clinic," one of the soldiers said. "We know you don't have the strength to do that. None of us can break out of that kind of reinforcement you had going on there, and the ship he arrived in is still here. He's somewhere on this spaceport."

"Maybe he stole a shuttle," Ted said, his voice a couple of decibels higher. Panic made his words come faster. "You know how crafty cyborgs are programmed to be. He's too smart to get trapped here."

"We're under orders," the soldier said. "We have authority to do whatever is necessary to make sure our objective is carried out."

Dasha and Rordan exchanged quick glances. "Maybe they'll think we already escaped," she whispered.

"If I was as smart as they think I am, we would've already," he replied.

Dasha ached to reassure him but didn't dare speak for fear of attracting attention.

"I don't know where they are," Ted said. "They were here, and now they're not. Isn't that good enough for you?"

"Weren't you military? You of all people should know that it isn't," the soldier said. "You left him in your lab at some point, and he broke out. Why won't you tell us more?"

The other soldier, silent for the entire exchange, looked up from the minicomp his gaze was trained on. "According to Mr. Best's bank account, he had a substantial deposit made around the time Rordan Alexander was known to have made his first visit here," he reported. "Half a million."

"Well, that's just perfect!" the first soldier replied. "It turns out there's a half-million tax to get off this spaceport alive!" To his comrade, he said, "Drain that account."

"No!" yelped Ted. He lunged for the soldier holding the minicomp, but both of them moved far faster than Ted. A brief whine of laser fire rang through the concourse. In a few seconds, the old man was lying on the deck motionless, blood pooling around his head.

Dasha bit back a cry and stepped back a little from the

catwalk railing, trying to put as much distance between herself and the scene unfolding through the grate. When Rordan reached for her, she leaned into him, needing the contact.

Another moment passed, and Ted didn't get up. The soldier who was interrogating him poked him with his boot. "He's dead," he said. "You had your weapon set to kill, you fuckstain."

"It was an accident," the other soldier replied. "It's not like Wilton's bounty hunter would've let him live if he got here first, anyway. And his money's transferred to us."

"Too late now. We have to find Alexander. I'm sure one of the other degenerates living here will tell us what they know."

The soldiers left Ted's body, stalking through the concourse as if he'd been nothing more than a bug under their boots.

Rordan motioned for Dasha to follow him, and she did, albeit on legs that were shaking. Even though she thought Ted was an opportunistic bastard, she still hadn't wanted to see him killed before her eyes.

She thought back to Janek Dalton breaking into her apartment and felt beads of sweat popping out along her brow and palms. The image of his dead face, eyes rolled back in his head, nearly made her stumble, and she gripped the railing to keep from collapsing to the catwalk.

Rordan sensed she was lagging behind and turned around. "Hey," he whispered. "I know what we saw back there was hard to watch, but we have to keep moving."

Tears leaked from the corners of her eyes. She tried to speak, but nothing came out.

"I promise we're going to get out of here," he said. "We'll get to the *Dragonfly,* or I'll find somewhere I can break into the spaceport's comp systems or a ship to hijack, *anything*. But we're getting out of this alive and never coming back to the Zone."

Dasha nodded, his words only minimally allaying her fears.

She *had* to believe him. She *needed* to believe him.

He hugged her, and Dasha eagerly leaned into him, needing his strength. He was solid, immovable, and over the odor of stale fuel, sweat, and sickly sweet darfin, she could detect the soap-clean scent of him. It was another reassurance she desperately needed.

Rordan released her, trailing a hand down her arm as he did so. Her skin prickled in a way that had nothing to do with the spaceport's chill. He started walking again, and she followed.

The catwalk branched off again, but an old comp panel was fused to the railing. Its cracked screen was dark, but its indicator light glowed yellow. "This is on standby," said Rordan excitedly.

"Are you sure you can do anything with it?" Dasha asked.

"If I can make a physical connection to a system on this spaceport, I could access everything," Rordan said. "We might not get another chance to do this." He ran his fingers over the panel. "I found a port I can connect to."

Dasha watched in morbid fascination as he pushed back the small cover on the port in his wrist, revealing a tiny, blue-colored prong. He set his wrist down and was about to plug himself into the comp panel when she placed a proprietary hand on his arm.

"Wait," she said. "How do we know you aren't going to, I don't know, scramble your brains or something?"

"I have surge protection." He considered the words for a couple of seconds. "That's a fucked-up thing to say."

"Rordan..."

"I think I used to swear a lot before I was a monk."

"Rordan!" Dasha's voice was a harsh whisper, and she lowered it. "I need you to come out of this in one piece, and for you to still be yourself." Could he permanently damage himself if he connected to the spaceport?

"Everything in life carries a risk," he said. "That was hammered into me in the military and at the temple, although the monks were more philosophical about it. We don't have a prayer of getting past those soldiers to the docks right now, not when I'm unarmed. There's only so much protecting I can do with my fists."

He stroked her cheek with callused fingertips. Goosebumps prickled along her skin. "I'll be fine," he promised.

The more Dasha clouded his plans with her fears, the longer this would take. She reached for his hand and squeezed it. "You'd better be."

Rordan kissed her with a ferocity and possession she hadn't expected, then, without another word, plugged his wrist into the comp panel.

CHAPTER 14

RORDAN, to the best of his recollection, had never electrocuted. But as he physically recoiled from the massive amount of data thrown at him by Spaceport 44's systems, he thought that might be what electrocution might feel like. Powerful currents raced through his body, setting every cybernetically enhanced part of his body on high alert.

Dimly, he was aware of Dasha's gasp of concern, but he blocked it out, trying to hone in on something tangible besides the numbers racing past his vision. He'd connected to the *Dragonfly*, but that was nothing like this: he could see the spaceport's schematics, pinpoint the hideouts its denizens were holed up in until the military left, find out details of the spaceport's life support infrastructure. He could see heat signatures denoting the humanoids on board, and there were far more people here than he initially assumed.

But all of it was a confusing mess, and it took a few minutes to figure out how to parse out each piece of information, hone in on it, and figure out what it meant.

The *Dragonfly* was still docked and hadn't been breached yet. Rordan was sure it was only a matter of time before someone took notice of how long she'd been there. He didn't remember a great deal about his cyborg-in-arms, Adam Johnston, but was sure he'd be angry if Rordan didn't return his ship in one piece.

There were a few other ships in the public docks as well; ones that looked deceptively unassuming, but Rordan could see they were armed to the teeth, none of their weaponry legal in the Zone. The military-issued shuttle that transported the soldiers was in the public dock as well. A pair of armed guards stood sentry at the airlock accessway.

That military shuttle model could transport up to ten people. Rordan had shadowy memories of being aboard them as a boy with his parents and later as a soldier, but he forced them out of his mind, focused on the information the spaceport was feeding him. That meant there was, at most, ten soldiers at the spaceport, and two of them were guards.

I can outsmart eight people.

But could he out-fight them? And not just out-fight them, but protect Dasha while he did so?

The worries about fights fell by the wayside when he spotted the code that led to the spaceport's communication systems. His heart skipped a beat at the realization, a sensation that he knew wasn't due to faulty cybernetics.

The spaceport comms seemed unmonitored, save for automatic alerts that raised a flag whenever a military craft was detected nearby. A single set of credentials was logged into the spaceport's systems, presumably linked to the person who'd sounded the alarm about the military raid.

Cautious excitement welled up in Rordan as he remotely accessed the *Dragonfly*'s comm system. He found a list of contacts on Kurkay-2 in the ship's computer but had no way of finding a way of writing a short message to them or recording a vid. He didn't want to spend too much time poking around the spaceport's and the *Dragonfly*'s systems in case someone noticed, so he didn't try to devise a way to make those comm systems work for him.

He could upload a voice message, though.

He cleared his throat, and when he spoke, his words were a hoarse whisper. "We're at Spaceport 44," Rordan said. "Dasha and I are both safe for now, but there's a military presence aboard, and they're looking for us." He paused, hoping the recipients could hear the sincerity and regret in his words. "I'm sorry for pulling her into this. I promise, I'll bring her back home safely."

He felt Dasha tug at his arm, dimly heard her whisper, "What the hell are you doing? Who are you talking to?"

Rordan didn't immediately respond. Instead, he downloaded the spaceport's blueprint, complete with its hiding places, before disconnecting himself from the computer. Waves of nausea and dizziness washed over him, and he leaned against the railing to keep from swaying. Slowly, his vision returned to normal.

The first sight he fixed on was Dasha and the worried look on her face. "Rordan," she said. "What just happened?"

Pain gripped his temples, so strong that it clouded his vision again. A memory fragment resurfaced at that moment: waking up in a barracks bunk, head muzzy after a night of drinking, but that flash of an old hangover had nothing on coming out whatever this was.

"Data overload," he mumbled. That was as good a name for it as anything.

"Rordan."

He swallowed, then took a deep breath of recycled air before blinking a couple of times, clearing his vision. "I'm all right," he said, but the croak in his voice betrayed him. Pain lanced itself, hot and sharp, down his limbs.

"Who were you talking to?"

"I was able to get into the *Dragonfly*'s comms," he said. "I recorded a message and sent it to everyone listed in Adam's comm file." His vision kept swimming, and he blinked again until Dasha came into focus. "I have the spaceport's blueprint and floor plan." He tried to tap his head, missed, then got it right on the second try.

"You do? Where are we?"

"We're in an old maintenance room," he said. His vision had cleared, and the pain in his legs lessened. "The spaceport has three of them. The one we walked through is the oldest, and this one was decommissioned a few years ago, although there are still a few components in use for backup purposes.

"The current maintenance room is on the other side of the spaceport and has biometric fortifications," he continued. "Almost useful has been stripped from this room."

"So, it's unlikely someone's going to come rushing in here to arrest or kill us?"

"I don't know." The spaceport's systems hadn't been able to tell him that. "And I don't know if the military won't come looking for us in here at some point. I think we should keep moving until we can safely get to the *Dragonfly*."

"Where should we go?"

"There's a small alcove in the current maintenance room," Rordan said. He brought up the spaceport's blueprint in his mind. He could see the closet-sized space tucked away off the catwalk that overlooked the energy core, dusty and windowless, its door nearly hidden by the room's darkness. It wouldn't be comfortable, but it was as decent a hideaway as they could get right now. As a bonus, that room was closer to the dock than they were now, and there were access tunnels branching off from it that would take them closer to the airlock accessway.

It was the only viable plan he could think of. He wished to the stars that he could get his hands on a weapon, if only for his own peace of mind.

"How far away is it?" Dasha asked.

"Just under seven hundred meters. We should get going."

She didn't argue, just grabbed his hand, and let him lead her away.

***

Rordan was quiet as they navigated their way over the catwalk, giving Dasha the unwelcome opportunity to ruminate over everything she'd done up until this point.

I had *to live in Westingtown on my own, instead of with Dad on the* Gray Ghost *or with Valenna and Anders. I would've been safer at their house.*

I killed Janek Dalton. That memory sent a shudder rippling through her. She wasn't sure she would ever come to terms with that.

I went exploring on Janek Dalton's ship and ended up hurtling through open space in an escape pod.

I followed Rordan out of my apartment and onto a ship we didn't have the right to take.

I have a stupid schoolgirl crush on a cyborg monk.

Dasha didn't know which thing, out of all of them, was the worst. Objectively, that dubious honor should've gone to her killing someone, but Janek Dalton was after her father. He hadn't cared a whit for Dasha.

Oh, Dad. Something twisted painfully in her chest when she thought of her father. She missed him fiercely.

I hope he's okay. He'd better not hop in a ship and try to come after me.

Even as the thought crossed her mind, she doubted Dr.

Caron would do such a thing himself. Not for lack of love for her, but because he possessed more common sense than he'd passed on to Dasha. He would certainly be aware of the risk crossing into the Zone posed, and he knew his limitations. He'd listen to the more experienced ex-soldiers and ex-mercenary waiting back in Westingtown.

And he'd want to kill Rordan when they got back.

That thought, at least, drew a small smile to her face. Rordan would probably let Dr. Caron try to dismantle him.

She was so caught up in her thoughts that she bumped into Rordan when he halted. "There," he whispered, pointing at a spot off the catwalk.

Had they really crossed to the other side of the spaceport already? "I'm really bad at reconnaissance," she muttered.

"What?"

"It's nothing." Seeing the skeptical look cross his face, she added, "I was daydreaming the whole way here, and I shouldn't have done that."

"No." His eyes, on night vision, flashed in her direction. "Even with my enhancements, I'm still not completely infallible."

"I know. I'm sorry." She tried to brush past him, to go to the spot he indicated, but he reached for her, stopping her.

"Don't be sorry," he said. "I still would've detected a threat. And if daydreaming gets you through this, then do it." He nodded his head to the hiding spot. "Let me check it out first. I've kept some reconnaissance abilities."

Dasha still followed him closely. The alcove turned out to be accessible through a door that was nearly hidden, blended into the wall. It was unlocked, and popped open with a push, springing back to reveal an empty closet barely wide enough for both of them.

A small, round viewport was set high into the wall,

revealing a glimpse of open space, although it offered nothing in the way of illumination. An emergency light glowed from the ceiling, highlighting the closet's dismal features, including a metal sink bolted haphazardly to the wall. A bucket holding a mop and a stack of small cleansing cubes rested against the wall next to the makeshift bathroom. When Dasha peered at them, she thought their dark stains resembled old blood. A shudder rippled through her.

Rordan had taken a few seconds to scope out the surrounding area and returned to the closet with a smile on his face. "I found another place to connect to the spaceport," he said. "I'll be able to monitor it when the military leaves, or whenever it's safe for us to get back to the *Dragonfly*. I still can't figure out a way to connect to their systems the way I can on the *Dragonfly*."

"Even an outlaw spaceport has security protocols."

"I'm sure I could bypass them if I knew more about my abilities, but I don't want to take any chances," Rordan said. "My presence would definitely set off alarms somewhere if I did that. When I'm connected through my wrist ports, I'm an... observer, I guess, is the best way to put it. I'm not actually part of the system the way I would be otherwise."

"That doesn't make sense. You're still connecting to the spaceport, but in a different way."

"It does," he insisted, but his tone was still patient. "If I hacked into the spaceport on a broadcast link, I'm turning myself into yet another computer among hundreds and would probably draw attention. When I use my wrist ports, I'm watching them, not a part of the system."

That explanation made a little more sense. Dasha nodded.

"The most important thing right now is getting you home safe," Rordan continued.

"No."

He tilted his head to the side, waiting for her explanation.

"You, too," Dasha said. "Both of us need to get home. Aren't you going to reconsider resuming your monk studies?"

"I was ready to take my vows, then I had four more years of study ahead before graduating to the intermediate stage," Rordan replied. "But I don't think I'm going back to the temple permanently. I'll want to return to say goodbye and thank Father Nelo and the others, but I don't think Glissat is the place for me anymore."

Dasha was aghast. "Why not? You don't have to give up monkhood just because you swore and kissed me. I won't tell anyone, and the stars and universe are supposed to be pretty forgiving."

Rordan didn't reply right away. Instead, he leaned against the wall and slid down until he was sitting on the floor. Dasha pretended not to notice the grime and did likewise.

Finally, after what felt like an interminable silence, he said, "It's not just that, although they are factors. Well, there's just *one* factor," he added. "I don't think the stars cared much when I cursed to maintain our cover and keep threats at bay."

Did he mean...? Dasha's heart pounded at the implication. Her breath caught, and she waited for him to continue.

But Rordan was quiet for an unsettling moment, probably gathering his thoughts.

Or preparing to break her heart.

"A monk's head has to be clear of all distractions, so we can better focus on the celestial and on our actions," he finally said. "I'm not having a crisis of faith, but I am questioning my role within that faith.

"I can't be a monk if I have romantic feelings for someone. The Order of the Benevolent Stars is as progressive as the Great Faith gets, but monks' celibacy is still a requirement."

Time seemed to stop for a moment as Dasha processed his words, stunned into silence. She knew Rordan was attracted to her, but a confession like that had been the furthest thing from her mind. She hadn't expected him to talk about *celibacy*, of all things.

But all she could muster was, "You have romantic feelings for me?"

His responding silence hung in the air, and she felt like an idiot.

"Because I have feelings for you, too," she added.

He answered that by taking her face in his hands. His dark eyes glinted in the dull light overhead, bright as stars, a promise in them she couldn't put words to but still felt all the same. Without a word, he kissed her with a ferocity that would have left her weak-kneed if she wasn't sitting. This was different than the other kisses they'd shared; there was a new intensity she hadn't experienced before.

It's Rordan, who he was before he lost his memory.

His hand found her shirt's hem, his calloused fingers lightly scoring her lower back. The light touch set every nerve in her body to attention, eliciting a gasp from her. Without meaning to, she pulled away to catch her breath.

Shock and anxiety furrowed a crease between Rordan's brows. He opened his mouth to speak, but Dasha cut him off.

"It's fine," she said. "I wasn't expecting that."

His expression didn't change.

"I like you," she said. "More than I should, given your being a monk."

"I don't think I can go back to that." Strangely, there wasn't a trace of regret in his voice.

"But if you do, and you broke your vow of chastity or whatever it is you agreed to, you'd hate yourself for it," Dasha said.

The look on his face shifted, became hungrier, a little feral. "I'd never regret anything with you. I think I wanted you the first time I saw you."

Her pulse beat a rapid tattoo, and a shaky laugh escaped her. "That isn't the kind of thing a monk's supposed to want."

"It isn't. But that doesn't change anything. You're smart and patient. If the stars had angels, you're what I imagined they look like. Of course I want you." He threaded his hands through hers, sharing his heat. "I'll never forgive myself for bringing you here."

"I *wanted* to go with you." Dasha squeezed his hands. "I'm here because I wanted to be. And I want you, too."

His face moved closer to hers, then he paused. Dasha could read the desire written across it, how it warred with indecision.

What the hell. We only live once.

As determined as they were to survive this, to get back to the Brava System, she knew there was a distinct possibility that things wouldn't unfold that way. And she would be damned if she was going to die without tasting him once.

She grabbed a fistful of his shirt and closed the distance between them. He responded eagerly, his teeth lightly nipping at her lower lip, the motion drawing another gasp from her.

Hampered by their awkward position, Rordan swiftly hoisted Dasha so she was straddling him, his back still against the wall. Excitement thrummed low in her belly at the contact, at the heat radiating from his body.

He surprised her when he tucked a strand of hair behind her ear, the gesture tender and somehow innocent. "I don't really remember how to do this," he whispered.

She leaned back a little as the implication hit her, knees still balanced on either side of him. "*Oh.*"

"I know I have, but I don't really remember it too much."

"That's okay," she said quickly. "I don't need to know the details."

"This is probably the worst possible timing."

"Yeah," she agreed. "But if someone busts through that door right now, would you regret it if we stopped?"

His pupils dilated, then shimmered. "By the stars, yes."

Her pulse pounded so hard she thought his cybernetic hearing was probably picking it up. She leaned into him, lips taking his as greedily as she could, her hands sliding under his shirt. They met hard muscle, skin scored with raised scars.

The motion drew a groan from his throat. He pulled away just enough to pull his shirt over his head, revealing his upper body. He tossed his shirt behind her. At her quizzical look, he said, "I don't want you to get dirty."

Dasha looked behind her, at his shirt haphazardly crumpled on the grimy floor, and laughed. "I appreciate the thought," she said. "But I don't think that'll be enough." She tightened her hold around his shoulders, drawing him closer to her. "And I don't care about getting dirty, anyway." Not if it meant sacrificing what could be her only chance to be with Rordan, danger be damned.

She stripped off her shirt, leaving it near his. She couldn't keep herself from preening a little as he raked an appreciative glance over her body, couldn't suppress goosebumps popping up along her skin that had nothing to do with the spaceport's perennial chill.

His mouth found hers again, his kiss gentle and teasing. His hand found her bra's seal and opened it, urging it down her arms until it joined their shirts on the floor. She maneuvered herself off his body until she was sitting on the floor, then lay back, taking him with her until his weight settled against her body, hips cradled against hers.

"Are you sure about this?" Rordan whispered in her ear.

"Very. Are you?"

"Yes, but I didn't imagine this kind of setting." He looked up and glanced around the closet as if to illustrate his point. "Definitely not on a bare floor."

"Who says this has to be the only time?"

The heat in his gaze told her he was thinking along the same lines. "Next time, it'll be a bed," he murmured into her ear. He caught her earlobe lightly in his teeth, sending a bolt of heat straight through her. "And it'll be romantic."

As much as she was looking forward to this, Dasha knew this wouldn't be especially romantic. Rordan seemed to be reading her thoughts, because they pulled at their clothes, unsealing and tugging waistbands down, mouths on each other's exposed skin.

In those moments, Dasha forgot about the danger they were in, that Rordan was a hunted man, even the spaceport's chill as his body heat warmed her. He stifled her sharp gasp with a fierce kiss as he entered her, his body greedy for her, insistent. And she loved it.

It wasn't until climax washed over each of them that Dasha was reminded of their reality. He leaned against her, his breath in her ear a reassurance that they were both still alive.

"Remember what I said about this not being romantic?" he whispered.

"I don't care about that."

"We should get dressed," he said. "We need to be ready for anything."

He was right, damn it. Dasha hated that fact.

They disentangled themselves from each other, with more than a little reluctance. He helped her to her feet, and they gathered their now-grimy clothes and dressed.

Rordan wrapped an arm around her waist, bringing her closer to him. "Thank you."

"No thanks necessary." A nervous giggle escaped her. "I just—I hope we haven't made things worse. That was a hell of a distraction."

"We haven't," Rordan said. "I said I'm going to get you home safe, and I meant that." Letting her go, he said, "I'm going to check on the spaceport's systems. There's a spot for me to link into it near here."

She didn't want him to leave the closet yet, but she understood.

It was a lot of work, keeping themselves alive long enough to get back over the border.

CHAPTER 15

BRINGING the *Gray Ghost* back to Kurkay-2 in one piece was more important than it had ever been, Cecily mused. She slid into the velvet-covered pilot's seat and activated the ship's engines, then brought up a pre-flight safety checklist.

Damn it, Rordan. I offered to bring you to Kurkay-2 in the first place after we left Omega-Three-Omega. Now I have to go back to the fucking Zone and bring you and Dasha back before both of you get killed.

Beside her, Jason ran down the list, ticking items off as Cecily readied for takeoff. "You're one hundred percent sure every necessary piece of medical equipment Dr. Caron needs is at the house?"

Cecily knew Jason was just being thorough, that he worried about their friends they were leaving behind on Kurkay-2, especially baby Sullivan, now a day and a half old. But now she doubted herself, despite Dr. Caron taking everything he could possibly need from her sickbay while they were away. "I'm sure," she said. "So was Dr. Caron. But if you remind me again, I'm going to have to go belowdecks and double-check to set my mind at ease."

The *Ghost* shimmied a little as she rose in the air, then

steadied. Cecily keyed in a course for the Zone border, and she temporarily forgot about Serena and Matthias's newborn son as she stared at the coordinates on her comp panel. She'd never intended to go back to the Zone ever again.

I really *hope no one's out to kill me.* She was out of practice when it came to defending herself with lethal force.

"I didn't want to make you doubt yourself," Jason continued. "I get nervous around babies. I'm not used to them. I'd rather leave Serena and Matthias over-prepared, you know?"

Cecily refrained from pointing out that Jason grew up in a deeply religious environment on a backwater planet that eschewed most technology. She assumed the modern conveniences they ignored included contraception, and that there had to be plenty of kids running around. It was a touchy subject for Jason. "I get it," she said. "And I'm the same around little kids." She thought about Rosie, Adam and Esme's four-year-old daughter. "Well, Rosie's smart," she amended. "I like her all right."

"Rosie can communicate," Jason said. "Babies cry and make you guess what's wrong with them."

"Good point. At least the wailing phase doesn't last that long, in the grand scheme of things."

In addition to its over-the-top luxury interior that only bore a passing resemblance to good taste, the *Ghost*'s best feature was the way she broke atmosphere. Her heavy air engine purring beneath their feet was the only indication that the ship was fighting gravity. Cecily would never stop appreciating that she wasn't pinned in her seat, trying not to puke on the deck as she would in a lesser ship.

Like Janek Dalton's *Raider*. What a horrible little ship.

But thinking of the *Raider* reminded Cecily again that they were heading into danger, and she brought up a report on the *Ghost*'s weapons array on her console. *Make the heavy air engine the second-best feature, instead.* Her cannons were primed, and she had a full complement of hand weapons in the locker below deck. She sneaked a glance at Jason, who was reading something on his own console.

"Should we change the *Ghost*'s ident code?" he asked. "Before we get to the border?"

Cecily had considered that before she mounted the rescue mission. To her shame, she still hadn't decided what would be the best course of action. "I don't know," she said. "There isn't a warrant for my arrest since I last checked, and the *Gray Ghost* is only known to other shady people. I can move between Bravan and Zone space freely with the current ident code. And I'm not worried about the military so much as any mercenaries I might've pissed off. I can only deal with one problem at a time right now."

"When did you last check for arrest warrants?"

"About one minute before I fired up the engines. And I'll check the galactic net again before we get to the border, just to be on the safe side."

The tension she hadn't noticed Jason holding in his shoulders relaxed. "Hey," she said softly, gaze meeting his. "I'm much more worried about Rordan and Dasha than I am about us. I know we can take care of ourselves."

"I kind of want to kill him right now." He ran his hand over his face, then stared at the forward viewscreen, at the stars before them. "I know he lost his memory, but you don't just up and fuck off with someone."

"You'll have to let Dr. Caron have the first crack at him. And for the record, I don't think Dasha went along unwillingly."

"I don't think she thought he was serious about leaving," he said. "Fuck it, I wished I knew the guy better, but he was the only one of us on Oh-Three-Oh who managed to keep to himself."

"He wasn't there as long as the rest of you, either."

"Yeah." A muscle ticked in his jaw. "It feels like every time something goes right for me or for us, the universe randomly throws a spanner in the works to wreck it." He got up from the copilot's seat and paced the bridge. "I like our life together, and I'm looking forward to being an honorary uncle, damn it. I'd rather be getting over my fear of babies right now."

There was one other thing that seemed to have slipped Jason's mind, the biggest foe to all the cyborgs living on Kurkay-2. *Everyone* appeared to have forgotten about it in the confusion Rordan and Dasha's exodus caused. But Cecily hadn't, and she was loathe to remind Jason of it right now.

But he needs to remember the other big threat we're facing in the Zone.

"Jason," she said.

The urgency in her voice halted him in his tracks.

Cecily hated what she had to say next. "We still have to think about Wilton Intergalactic Fluid Technology," she said. "They're still after the cyborg tech."

As the ship gracefully raced for the Zone border, Cecily was treated to an array of swear words from Jason, in multiple languages, many of which she'd never heard before.

Rordan stayed awake all night, Dasha's head in his lap as she slept.

Occasionally, he touched a glossy strand of sun-bleached dark hair, alternating between reassurance and anxiety by the rhythm of her breath while slept on. She was alive, she was safe for the time being and under his protection, but her presence still posed a massive risk to both of them, especially her.

He cared about her too much to let anything happen to her.

They'd managed to hole up in the cleaning closet overnight, and Rordan guessed they'd been in there for about ten hours. *Would've been nice if I had a chronometer built into my cybernetics. Seems like a logical thing for a cyborg to have.* Thus far, any cybernetic advantages Rordan had seemed to be limited to excessive strength and speed, and the ability to connect with comp systems. All of which were useful, hardly worth killing him and reverse-engineering his tech.

And I can operate on very little sleep. That was a blessing, too.

One of the human needs he still had made itself evident as his stomach growled, loud enough to wake Dasha. She raised her head, a little confused. "What the hell was that?" she asked sleepily. Without waiting for him to answer, she looked around the closet. "Oh. We're still here."

"And we'll get out of here soon," Rordan said.

She lifted herself to a sitting position and leaned back against the wall, shoulder to shoulder with him. "Sorry," she said. "I know you've been awake all night. I don't want to start the day off with complaints."

"Why not? My stomach did."

His attempt at lightening the mood must have worked because that coaxed a smile from Dasha. "Have you heard anything?"

He shook his head. "Not a peep. Although I haven't left the closet since we got here."

The words reminded him again of what they'd shared since they took to hiding out in the closet, an event he'd mulled over through the night. Judging from the blush that tinted her cheeks, she was thinking of the same thing.

"I had fun last night," Dasha said. "I know it's a weird thing to say right now, but I did."

Rordan laced his fingers through hers, focused on her warmth. He thought he could feel the rush of blood through her veins, her very life force. "I did, too," he said. He squeezed her hand, was reassured by her gesture in kind. "I'm going to check the spaceport's systems," he said. "I'll be back in a couple of minutes."

"What if someone's out there?" Dasha asked.

"I don't have most of the sensory abilities the other cyborgs have," Rordan replied. Some of the others could detect life signs and heat signatures through walls, and could even pick up on human body temperatures. "But my hearing is in top-notch shape. I would've heard anyone approaching."

Dasha nodded but didn't seem mollified. After everything that had happened over the last couple of days, Rordan didn't blame her, much as it pained him to admit that.

He brought his face to hers in a kiss. "I'll be fine," he promised.

"You don't have anything to defend yourself with."

"There's no one out there," he said. Even if he came across a working weapon, he wasn't sure he would remember in time to correctly use it without getting either of them injured. His muscle memory was returning erratically, and he didn't trust it.

"I believe you," she said. "Just don't get yourself hurt, okay? I need you."

Hearing that statement made Rordan's heart skip a beat, and he knew it wasn't a flaw in his cybernetics. "I'll be back before you know it."

With a final kiss, he rose to his feet and unlocked the closet door. He opened it a crack, letting in cool air, and listened.

The only sound that came back to him was the hum and grind of the machinery that kept the spaceport running. The only odor was that of grimy recycled air and the faint smells of sweat and fuel that had seeped into every nook and cranny.

He opened the door wider and stuck his head out. The catwalk was exactly as it had been the night before.

Rordan crept out of the closet, taking care to close the door behind him, and found the nearby spot where he could connect to the spaceport's systems. He pressed his wrist into the available port, a console that had once been used to check life support readings, and waited.

Now that he'd done it a couple of times, he didn't feel so physically overwhelmed by the data rushing past his vision. He could pick out what he needed to know, had re-trained himself to hone in on minute details. Relief poured through him when he saw that the military presence had lifted, the raid was over, and it looked like life was returning to normal for the people aboard the spaceport.

Except Ted. Messages shared between residents that Rordan was able to pick up revealed that Ted's body was left in the spaceport's morgue. He didn't know what happened to people who died at Spaceport 44 and didn't want to explore further. The military was gone, the *Dragonfly* still in dry dock and untouched, and it didn't appear that anyone was looking for them anymore.

The route he'd chosen to take through the spaceport's maintenance tunnels and hidden accessways was still empty, too. It looked like he and Dasha would be able to leave this place unscathed.

He disconnected his wrist and blinked, clearing his vision. A smile bloomed across his face, and he quickly walked back to the closet, a feeling resembling giddiness putting a small spring in his step.

He was struck with the memory of a furtive, hurried walk across the lawn of his childhood home, excited to be out of the house on a beautiful day. He was on his way to a fort he constructed in the woods bordering the yard. His parents and the house's staff didn't know about his hideaway, and he loved having the space to play in. As far as he knew, his parents never discovered it, either.

Huh. What a weird thing to remember.

But it brought back warm, fuzzy feelings at least.

He slipped back into the closet, where Dasha immediately threw her arms around him. Her shoulders heaved, and when she pulled away, he saw tears streaking her face. "You came back," she said, her voice a hoarse whisper. "You're okay."

"I said I would be," Rordan replied. "I promised I'd be okay, and I am." He squeezed her hands. "And it's safe for us to get back to the *Dragonfly*. The military's gone, and life's gone back to what passes for normal here."

Hope lifted the corners of her mouth and brought a sparkle back to her eyes. "Really?"

"Yeah. And I don't know about you, but I'm starving and looking forward to eating whatever protein cubes are on the ship." He inclined his head to the door. "Let's go."

He led her back to the catwalk, and from there, to the maintenance tunnel that would bring them closer to the docks. The temperature dropped as they walked, a sure sign they were closer to freedom than ever.

Could it really be this easy? Did I outsmart the military?

Pride surged in him, an unfamiliar feeling since he became a monk. He didn't have the useful cybernetics his fellow Omega-Three-Omega soldiers had, but he could still download a spaceport's blueprints into his head, plot a course, and get himself and Dasha back to relative safety.

He stopped at a rusty square cut into the catwalk, a trapdoor the blueprint indicated would be here. He lifted its lid, both of them cringing at its protesting squeal, revealing a bare metal ladder. The blueprint said it descended four and a half meters to an old airlock control room, stripped out for parts. From there, they could leave the control room, enter the main corridor to the docks, and finally get aboard the *Dragonfly*.

Rordan glanced at Dasha, who surprised him with a smile.

"It's a good thing I'm not afraid of heights," she said and motioned for the ladder.

He placed a proprietary hand on her arm, stopping her. "Let me go first."

"Oh. Good point."

Rordan didn't hear anything around or below them, and he quickly descended the ladder. Glancing around the empty room, its panels ripped out like they'd been taken in a hurry, he confirmed that they were alone.

Dasha followed him, then when her feet touched the deck, he gripped her hand again.

Stars and universe, it felt so good to not be alone anymore.

The door was manual, dull-gray metal badly dented by the stars knew how many fights and tussles. Scorch marks from laser weapons scored its interior, indicating older, deadlier fights that had taken place in the room's small confines at one point. Cognizant of the dangers that could be lurking in the airlock corridor, Rordan pressed his ear to the door and listened. All that reported back to him was the sputtering whoosh of an air recycler. Rordan gingerly eased the door to its side, and, with a knot in his stomach, glanced into the corridor.

Empty. *Thanks be to the stars.* He could even see the door that led to their dock from here. Turning his head, he whispered, "It's clear. Let's go."

Dasha didn't need to be told twice.

Both of them bolted, footsteps echoing on the metallic deck until they reached the dock door. Its lock was numeric, a random code sent to the *Dragonfly* when they requested permission to dock, and Dasha entered it now. The lock groaned before whirring its assent, and the dock door opened.

The *Dragonfly* was exactly where they left her, and it appeared untouched. Relief coursed through Rordan, and he realized he hadn't let himself think about what they would do if they found her disabled or stolen.

The ship's exterior palm lock responded to Rordan's handprint, and its rampway extended. They ran inside, and Dasha recalled the ramp while Rordan raced for the bridge.

He activated the ship's engines. Static crackled through the bridge's comm system, and a sleepy voice said, "The fuck you're doing? Who's out there?"

"Open the airlock," Rordan commanded.

"You know what time it is, numbnuts?"

"Open the airlock!" he repeated. "Or may the stars help us both, I'll break out!"

He hoped it wouldn't come to that. He doubted the *Dragonfly* could do such a thing, and even if it could, Adam Johnston would be very upset if he returned his ship half-destroyed.

Adam Johnston was going to be very upset, anyway.

"Early," the voice said, answering his own question about the time. "It's fucking early. Give me a minute, I'll open the airlock. You better not have anything living in your dock right now, because I don't follow safety protocols when I'm woken up by a lowlife fuckface like you."

Rordan looked at Dasha. "Am I a fuckface?" He set a course for the Zone border.

"Not in the least."

To the speaker, Rordan said, "Go for it. And maybe you should find a proper bed to sleep in, instead of a controller's booth."

"Maybe *you* should..."

The controller's threat was cut off by static. The airlock door opened, and, more roughly than Rordan was expecting, the *Dragonfly* was sucked into space.

He and Dasha waited for a tense moment until the spaceport's airlock door resealed itself, and the *Dragonfly* glided into space. The only sound was the engine's purr and the faint whirr of the life support system.

Dasha was the first to speak. "You did it!" she shrieked and threw herself into Rordan's arms.

He was happy to receive her. "*We* did it."

"It was mostly you," she said. "Oh, my God, I can't believe we got away!"

"And the stars," Rordan murmured into her hair. He looked at the forward viewscreen and was comforted by the sight of the stars. *Thank you, universe. I will not squander this second chance at a new life.*

Third chance, he mentally corrected himself. Taking monk's vows technically counted as his second chance.

He tore his gaze away from the stars so he could take in Dasha: memorize every sun-kissed freckle on her nose, every lash around her dark eyes. He never thought she looked more beautiful.

Like the angel I thought she was the first time I saw her.

And now he was free to kiss her, just as he wanted to when he saw her stick her head out of that escape pod.

She met him eagerly, tongue demanding entrance to his mouth in a motion that made him forget everything that had happened at Spaceport 44. He was ready to let the ship guide them while he took her back to the captain's cabin, but another bodily need reminded him it needed tending to.

"Breakfast," he said.

Her eyelids were still half-hooded with lust, but she said, "Right."

The galley had, as Rordan guessed, protein cubes, and they each ate one. He wasn't even bothered by its dusty, vaguely fishy taste; all that mattered was that in a short time, they would be back in the Brava System, back to safety.

And he was never leaving her side.

Before they could split the remaining protein cube, a klaxon trilled throughout the ship.

"Oh, no," said Dasha, but Rordan was already running for the bridge.

Her footsteps sounded behind him, and she nearly crashed into him as he stared at the viewscreen. A dark, oblong-shaped vessel appeared in the starfield. The comm system lit up with a hail request.

"Is that military?" Dasha asked.

"I don't think so." Rordan acknowledged the hail. "Captain here."

"Power down and prepare to be boarded," a crackly male voice said through the speaker.

"What?" breathed Dasha.

"No," said Rordan into the speaker. "Leave us be, or I'll be forced to take action."

"Absolutely not, Captain Alexander," the voice replied. Amusement tinged his words, even through the static. "I've been looking for you for a long time. You can cooperate with me, or I can blow you out of the stars and let Wilton reverse-engineer what's left of your bolts."

Wilton.

The water company.

Another hail sputtered through the comm. "Stand down, *Dragonfly,*" a different voice ordered. "Remain in place, by order of the Zone military."

For a horrifying moment, time seemed to stand still.

Rordan forced himself to look at Dasha. She stared at the viewscreen, unmoving, face frozen in horror.

He should have known it was too bloody easy getting off that spaceport.

I've killed both of us.

CHAPTER 16

"DON'T MOVE," one of the voices said through the comm. Dasha couldn't tell who it was, and at this point, she doubted the detail was important.

Her vision dimmed, the dark ship blurred on the viewscreen. She thought it was advancing toward the *Dragonfly* until Rordan's arms circled her. "Stay with me," he said. "Take a deep breath."

She did as he said, then blinked. Her vision returned to normal, and she realized that she'd nearly fainted dead away on the deck. "Thank you," she said hoarsely, righting herself.

"They *let* us get away," Rordan said bitterly. "I should've known we escaped too easily. Dasha, I'm sorry."

Was that apology a sign of his impending surrender? "No," she said, her voice louder than she intended. "We're not going with either of them." She slid into the captain's chair. "There has to be a way for us to get away. It's a huge fucking galaxy, and there are only two ships." She scanned the command screens, hoping for a button that would launch exploding torpedoes, anything that would take down a well-shielded military vessel and bounty hunter ship. "We've come too far to let the military or Wilton Intergalactic take you."

She tapped at the screen until the weapons array prompt appeared. Before she could do anything further, Rordan pulled her up.

"I'll deal with this," he said, sliding into the seat. Dasha's legs shook under her, barely keeping her up, and she gripped the back of the pilot's seat as Rordan guided the ship away from the area.

Enraged protests garbled from the comm, but he ignored them. Heart in her throat, Dasha watched the viewscreen as the dark-colored ship advanced. She couldn't see the military vessel but knew it had to be nearby.

The *Dragonfly* violently tilted aft, and she crashed to the deck. "Damn it!" she cried out. Her left knee and hip throbbed. Tears pricked at her eyes, not just from the impact but from the fear coursing through her.

The ship banked hard to starboard, and Dasha gave up trying to stand for the time being. She slid against the wall, head and shoulder meeting pitted metal, but thankfully not as hard as her first fall was. She didn't focus on that and instead fixed her attention on Rordan.

He was still seated, gaze intent, and eyes flicking between the forward viewscreen and the command console in front of him. She realized he'd interfaced with the ship. It dipped and lurched forward, then took off at a speed Dasha didn't think it was capable of.

The *Dragonfly* tilted again, this time to port, and she skidded across the deck. "How are you still sitting upright?" she yelped.

"I don't know," Rordan said. "And I don't know how I remember to do this, only that I can. I can't be distracted right now."

What could she do to help him? She looked around the cockpit but knew there was nothing she could do at the moment.

I'm going to get out of this, and I'm going to teach at that school again. They said they'd be happy to take me back when my fake family emergency is over.

She envisioned herself in her old classroom, surrounded by six-year-olds, sun streaming through the floor-to-ceiling windows. She thought about the big holodisplay in the middle of the room, projecting images of the humanoid body, the kids' fascination with spines and leg bones, and wiped away tears.

She thought about the treehouse she'd shared with her father. *Oh, Dad, I miss you the most. I love you so much.*

The *Dragonfly* bucked, then continued in God knew whatever direction it was headed in. She dearly hoped it was the border.

No wonder Dad never wanted to come back to the Zone.

"Dasha? Rordan?"

The voice coming from the comm was female and familiar. "Oh, my God," Dasha said. "I think it's Cecily!"

Hope surged in her, and she rose to her feet, careful to maintain her balance. "Rordan!" she said.

He didn't look at her, keeping his focus trained on getting away from the other ships. They weren't visible on the viewscreen, but not much was, given the incredible speed at which Rordan had the *Dragonfly* moving. "I heard," he said. He glanced down at the navigation panel. "She's twenty-one minutes away, at the *Gray Ghost*'s current speed. No, now it's eighteen minutes."

That meant Cecily was gaining on them, had probably already seen they were in trouble. Dasha looked at the panel and saw colored dots with ident codes transposed over them, along with their current speeds and distance in minutes and seconds. Their pursuers were alarmingly close, about six and eight minutes away.

The dot that was furthest away picked up speed.

"Could someone answer?" said Cecily. "Let me know you're alive."

"Damn it," Dasha said. She slapped at the comm's speaker. "We're okay," she said.

"No, we aren't," Rordan said.

"We're alive," Dasha clarified. "And we're in trouble."

"I can see that. Hang on, I'm almost there."

Dasha looked back at navigation. The *Gray Ghost* was now eleven minutes away.

Eleven minutes. They could hold out that long, couldn't they?

"Both ships' weapons arrays are hot," Rordan said. His voice was bleak. "The bounty hunter has an EMP primed." He let go of the controls and grabbed Dasha's hands. "I don't know if we're going to make it." Desolation tore at his voice, and a corresponding pain gripped her heart. "Our laser cannon can't compete with an EMP."

She didn't know the magnitude of damage an electromagnetic pulse could do to the *Dragonfly* and didn't want to find out. She shook her head. "No," she said. "Cecily's nearly here. We just have to keep moving."

"We have no viable weapons, no subspace engine..."

"Keep moving!" she screamed. Rordan flinched.

"I have a course set for the border," he said. "If something happens to me, keep on this course. And I love you."

His metallic eyes fixed on hers, and for a second, Dasha's body went numb. "What?"

The *Dragonfly* jumped, and for a second, every light on the bridge seemed to glow. Rordan's eyes went wide, then blank. He tilted to the side and slid out of the pilot's seat to the deck.

The EMP!

"Rordan!" She shook his shoulder, but he didn't respond. He stared at her blankly, eyes unblinking.

But he was breathing. He was still alive.

"Dasha," said Cecily through the comm. "One of the ships sent out an EMP. Is Rordan all right?"

"He's still breathing, but that's it."

Cecily interrupted her. "No time for chitchat, but—shit! Sorry," she said. "He's out cold but breathing?"

"Yeah."

"You need to get the *Dragonfly* moving again for now. I'm almost there, okay?"

With a start, Dasha realized the *Dragonfly* had slowed down. When she looked at the controls, she saw the course Rordan plotted, waiting on the captain's confirmation. She slipped into the pilot's seat and tapped the controls to start the ship again, and it picked up speed, slower than before.

Now what?

With a longing glance at Rordan, she took her place in the captain's seat and tried to get a better feel for what was in front of her, what she had to do.

"Stay alive," she murmured. "I can keep us alive."

The course Rordan plotted included a designated speed, which Dasha left as it was. A warning flashed on the screen: "Ship rebooted. Do you want to continue the course without a full systems scan?"

"Shit," Dasha said. "I guess so."

A glance at navigation told her the enemy ships were each four minutes away. The *Gray Ghost*, six.

"Rordan," she said. She leaned down and shook him again. "You have to wake up. You can't leave me hanging with a love declaration and then fall over."

He didn't move.

"God damn it!" she wailed. "I think I love you, too, and we're going to die!"

The navigation screen was engulfed in a red wash of color, and the *Dragonfly*'s bridge lights flickered again. Nausea crested over Dasha, and she thought she might puke on the deck.

Big letters marched across the command console: SYSTEM SHUTDOWN. REBOOTING IS COMMENCING.

When the navigation screen cleared, it revealed stilled dots, save for one moving at a rapid clip toward the *Dragonfly*. She dearly hoped it was the *Ghost*.

The engine sputtered, and the ship started moving again. As it did so, she noticed another dot had regained its mobility, too.

Which ident code belonged to who?

The screen flashed again: WEAPONS ONLINE.

The *Dragonfly*'s laser cannon was one step removed from being completely useless, but it would have to do. One of the ships was closing in faster than the other, and she wished like hell she could tell who it was. She tapped on the blinking dots, but all she could pick up was model numbers, specs, and ident codes. Nothing that indicated the ship's names.

But one was definitely larger than the other. The *Gray Ghost* was a large ship, a converted luxury passenger transport. The bounty hunter that was after them was traveling in something smaller and less conspicuous.

And the smaller vessel definitely closer to the *Dragonfly* right now, catching up and surpassing the speed of the *Gray Ghost*.

It took a precious few seconds to do it, but she managed to bring up the image of the closer ship on the forward viewscreen.

It glided toward her, small, dark, and sleek. It was definitely the bounty hunter.

He was a minute away. Dasha activated the laser cannon, directing it through the aft weapons tube, and, guided by the command suggestions, aimed it best as she could at the approaching vessel.

The *Dragonfly* shook as the cannon fired. A few seconds later, another message appeared on the screen.

TARGET HIT.

Dasha's blood ran cold. Instead of elation that she'd successfully bought the *Dragonfly* some time, all she could think about was that she killed another person. A wordless cry of anger, shame, and frustration escaped her.

No. Don't think about that right now!

She looked at Rordan, still lying wide-eyed on the deck, motionless save his slow, steady breathing.

"Dasha?"

Cecily's voice crackled through the comm. Dasha latched on to it like it was a lifeline, the only thing keeping her sane. Maybe it was. "Cecily?" Her voice broke. "I think I killed someone again."

"No, you didn't," Cecily said. "You disabled the *Rook* and bought us some time to get away, but I don't know how long the *Rook* will be out for. And," she added, "The *Rook* sent out the EMP. It disabled the military ship, Jason, and Rordan. Both ships are now disabled."

"They'll recover, won't they?"

"Yes." Impatience colored Cecily's words. "But we need to get away before they do that."

"How come the *Dragonfly* and *Ghost* are still operational?"

"Adam and I installed precautions against EMPs, although they didn't work for actual cyborgs. I'll be in your range in a minute, and I'm going to extend a tractor and haul you with me until we get to the border. Sit tight." She paused. "You saved your ass when you fired that cannon. The *Rook* was a lot closer than I would have liked." The comm crackled again, then went silent.

"Dasha?"

Rordan's voice was strained as if it were painful. Dasha was on the deck at his side in an instant.

"Oh, my God," she said, touching his cheek. "Are you all right? There was an EMP."

Rordan swallowed, cringed, and spoke again. "It disabled electrical systems, including me. I can't move yet."

"I can help you up."

"No," he said. "Leave me here for now. It'll all come back in time. I heard everything." He coughed. "You did well."

Even though she was still scared out of her mind for him, Dasha still warmed with his praise. "Thank you."

He coughed again, swallowed. "And I meant what I said before. I love you."

His eyes shone, although if it was due to emotion, his cybernetics rebooting, or a combination of both, Dasha couldn't tell. It wasn't important, anyway. "I love you, too," she said.

Any response he might have offered was interrupted when a clunk sounded above them, sending vibrations running through the ship. Cecily said through the comm, "Don't worry, it's just me. Hang on, I think this is going to be the fastest trip to the border I've ever made."

Dasha reached for Rordan's hand and squeezed it. Ever so gently, he squeezed back.

CHAPTER 17

RORDAN COULDN'T RELAX—PHYSICALLY or mentally—until the *Dragonfly* safely crossed the Bravan border.

Telling Dasha he loved her was only the first thing he needed to say. Everything else would have to wait until they landed, and possibly after he had the shit beaten out of him by her father. He would certainly do the same in Dr. Caron's position.

He remembered *everything*.

The EMP had jostled something loose and spilled every memory he had before his ghastly black market surgery through his mind. He remembered his childhood on Garshan, his aloof parents, their disappointment in him when he didn't turn to a life of academia after earning his philosophy degree.

The battles on the Bravan-Zone border returned, along with the memories of fallen comrades, the smell of blood in the air. His own injuries, and a man who introduced himself as Dr. Jacoby, who could help him.

The persistent chill of Omega-Three-Omega, the sense of dread there that never abated. The fear of a painful "punishment" from Dr. Jacoby for not performing one of the doctor's sadistic tests to his satisfaction. The loss of his voice as a means of control. His fellow cyborgs there, his reluctance to join their private broadcast link and spill his proverbial guts to them.

He wasn't able to dwell on his time on Oh-Three-Oh just yet. It was still too painful, too raw to process. Instead, as he lay on the deck, he watched Dasha navigate the *Dragonfly* as she landed the ship.

She received some direction from the *Gray Ghost*, augmenting her piloting knowledge she'd picked up from shuttles. It was bumpier than he was used to when they broke atmosphere, but she still managed to land the *Dragonfly* without incident.

And by then, Rordan could stand on his own.

The first thing he did was reach for Dasha, rising from the pilot's seat, and kiss her. His body heated in a way that had nothing to do with the effects of the EMP, but a sharp, shooting pain his lower back had him reluctantly pulling away.

"You mean everything to me," he murmured in her ear. "I will never go a day without thanking the stars and universe that you came into my life."

"Even though I wrecked your monk career?" Her voice was breathless, and it pleased him to know he had that effect on her.

"Father Nelo will understand. There are other ways of honoring the stars than being a monk."

He lurched, his body readjusting to gravity and recovering from the EMP, and Dasha helped steady him. "We need to get to Valenna and Anders's place," she said, changing the subject. "My father and the others will want to know we're okay. Let's get in a flitter and see them now."

Rordan nodded. "I have a lot of groveling to do, to everyone."

Dasha led him to the airlock and unlocked the exterior door. "Then let's get started."

It was evening, nearly fully dark, by the time they reached Valenna and Anders's home. The *Gray Ghost* had landed in her usual spot on the edge of the property in an unused field; seeing it there reminded Dasha of Serena and her pregnancy.

And when she thought of Serena, she thought of her father, acting as Serena's physician.

Every light in the farmhouse was blazing as they walked up to the front door, which was thrown open before she could knock. Valenna nearly launched herself in their direction, wrapping her arms around Dasha in a fierce hug. Before she could do the same to Rordan, Dasha put a hand on her arm, stopping her.

"I'm not at one hundred percent yet," Rordan said by way of explanation.

Dr. Caron was waiting in the foyer when they stepped into the house. Dasha had never seen him this way before: his silver hair mussed, red-rimmed eyes shadowed, his laugh lines more pronounced. He looked much older than his sixty-two years.

And very, very angry.

Gaze fixed squarely on Rordan, he snarled, "You utter *bastard*."

"Dad!" said Dasha sharply. "Don't get mad at him. *Both* of us left. He didn't kidnap me."

Dr. Caron's fists hung at his sides, but they flexed and relaxed a couple of times. It took a few seconds for him to notice his daughter, and when he did, his expression softened somewhat.

That was all the encouragement she needed. She left Rordan's side to embrace her father, who seemed to collapse against her in relief. "You're all right," he breathed. "I can't tell you how worried I was when I found out he took you."

"Dad," she said again. "He didn't take me. I volunteered

to go with him." She glanced back at Rordan, who looked apologetic and a little terrified of Dr. Caron. "I thought I could talk him out of it, but I couldn't, and I worried about him going off to Spaceport 44 alone, and... well, we're back. The military didn't get us, and neither did a bounty hunter."

Dr. Caron's eyes narrowed. "Cecily said something about that, yes. I was helping to revive Jason when she mentioned it."

"Is he okay?" she asked.

"A little stiff, but he recovered nicely from the EMP," he replied. To Rordan, he said, "I see you have, as well."

"Yes, sir."

"How are you feeling?"

Despite the professional question, Dasha heard unease in her father's voice. She could tell by his more relaxed stance that he believed her when she said she went with Rordan of her own accord, but he was still upset. While his hands stayed by his side, they kept forming into fists. She suspected it would take a while for him to fully accept Rordan.

Rordan nodded. "A little stiff like Jason, but the flitter ride here helped with that, I think." He took a deep breath. "And all of my memories are back."

Valenna caught Dasha's eye, and she mouthed, "Holy shit!"

That bit was news to Dasha. "They did?"

"After the EMP," he explained. "They were already coming back, and the black market surgeon who worked on me said they would return in time, but..." He tapped his head. "They're all here."

Dr. Caron nodded, his professional veneer restoring itself. "So, you spoke with the person who operated on you and induced amnesia?"

"I did, and I'll tell you about it later," Rordan replied.

"He's dead now." At the sight of Dr. Caron's upraised eyebrows, he added, "I didn't kill him. The military did."

Dasha could see her father was getting worked up again. "We'll tell you everything later," she promised. "We wanted to come here and show you we're okay."

"And you have to meet Sullivan," Valenna interjected.

Sullivan? Did that mean…?

"Serena had her baby!" Valenna announced. "After you two left. He and Serena are in the living room. Want to meet them?"

"Are you nuts? Of course."

Valenna led them to the living room, where Serena and Matthias were huddled together on the couch, a tiny form wrapped in a blanket held in Serena's arms. Both of them looked tired, but Dasha had never seen Serena look happier.

"They're back," Valenna whispered. "And they want to meet your little guy."

Serena rose and held out her tiny sleeping son. "His lungs are incredible," she said softly. "Not that I'm complaining, and I'm sure you'll get to hear him wail at least once tonight. We're both healthy, and that's the important thing." She looked down at Sullivan, clearly besotted. "He's more precious than I thought he'd be."

Dasha was itching to hold him. "May I?" she asked.

Serena nodded, and they squished on the couch together. Sullivan stirred a little when Serena handed him off but stayed asleep. "How are you doing?" she asked Matthias.

"The love of my life and our son are healthy and happy," Matthias replied. "Sullivan is also the cutest baby that's ever existed, if I may say so myself." He beamed at Serena. "Therefore, I'm happy, too."

Adam and Esme walked into the living room from the kitchen. Rordan flinched.

"Corporal Johnston," Rordan said stiffly. "My memory's returned, and I owe you an apology."

From her spot on the couch, Dasha heard Adam and Esme's daughter, Rosie, ask about an extra piece of cake. Esme turned her head and said, "In a minute, sweetheart."

"I returned the *Dragonfly* to her spot in the shipyard," Rordan continued. "She's in the same shape she was in when I took her. *Stole* her," he corrected himself. "Her cannon was fired, and I'll pay to have its ammo resupplied."

Esme returned to the kitchen. "Yes, you can have another piece of cake," she said. "A *small* one. That's a lot of sugar before bedtime."

Adam finally spoke. "I'd hardly call a laser cannon a 'weapons array.' And I'm really glad the EMP protection wasn't a waste of money."

Some of the tension in the room dissipated.

"I'm still sorry," Rordan said. "What I did was inexcusable, memory loss or no. It went against everything I believe in, based on my morals before and after I was in the military and especially when I joined the Order of the Benevolent Stars."

Adam nodded. "I get it. And this is forgivable, even if it's extremely weird." He barked out a harsh, short laugh. "Everything about this is fu—" He glanced behind him in the kitchen, presumably remembering his four-year-old daughter was in earshot. "Everything about this is weird," he amended. He added, "I'm usually really good about watching my language." Looking in the kitchen again, he said, "My wife and daughter are here if you'd like to meet them."

"I would."

He was visibly relieved at the invitation and followed Adam to the kitchen. Dasha looked down at the sleeping bundle in her arms and reluctantly gave him back to Serena.

"I'll be back soon," she promised. "I still want to snuggle him."

Matthias held out his arms to Serena, who passed Sullivan to him. "He's very snuggle-able."

Dasha had never seen the kitchen so full of people before: Valenna and Anders, Cressida, Adam and Esme, Cecily, and Jason. Adam and Esme's daughter, Rosie, sat at the table, oblivious to everything except the small slice of cake in front of her.

And Rordan, standing next to Adam, and her father.

Lukas strode into the kitchen from the back door, a patched-together thincomp in his hand. "My father contacted me," he said. "About twenty minutes ago. I've been outside talking to him."

Everyone turned to look at Lukas. Cressida immediately reached for him, concern across her face. Dr. Caron wore the same expression. Lukas didn't like to speak about his father, let alone to him.

"He said he found out about Wilton Intergalactic Fluid Technology wanting cyborg tech," Lukas continued. "He found out about the bounties they put out for anyone who could bring in a cyborg, living or dead, and the military made a formal announcement, galaxy-wide, on the galactic net an hour ago." He laid the thincomp on the table.

Oblivious to his announcement, Rosie hopped down from her chair. "Can I see the baby?"

Serena now lingered in the doorway. "Go ahead," she said. "He's with Uncle Matthias."

Rosie took off, and Serena took her place at the table. A couple of bites of Rosie's cake remained on the plate, and Serena said, "Does anyone mind if I eat this?"

Valenna and Esme looked at her, aghast. "I have half a cake left if you want a fresh piece," Valenna said.

"I'm not bothered by kid germs," Serena breezily replied and ate the rest of Rosie's cake.

"You're getting right into motherhood," Esme said.

Lukas tapped the thincomp screen. "This is important."

An image of an elderly man was superimposed over the cracked screen. He wore the stark black uniform of the Zone military, and still bore an imposing countenance despite his age. He bore a striking resemblance to Lukas.

"On behalf of the Zone's military, I am officially discrediting all rumors of cyborg and cybernetic research and activity," the man said. "Effective immediately, if anyone in Zone space pursues this research, issues bounties for suspected cyborgs, or harasses anyone based on their suspicion of being a cyborg, however unfounded, they will face severe legal and financial penalties. Let me be clear." He leaned closer to the visualizer's lens. "The military's cybernetic research program was discontinued many years ago following many cyborg failures. Aside from the use of artificial organs and limbs when medically necessary, cybernetic enhancement is illegal. *Cyborgs do not exist*." He glowered at the visualizer before continuing. "We have been made aware of corporations who have pursued this prohibited and inhumane research, and they will be dealt with to the fullest extent of the law."

The image winked out.

The kitchen was silent, the only noise the murmur of conversation in the living room between Matthias and Rosie about the baby.

"My father told me this was being broadcast," Lukas finally said. "He told me in confidence that Wilton is being sanctioned and sold off to another conglomerate immediately."

"How did he know about Wilton's pursuit?" Rordan asked.

Dasha knew. She turned to her father, who lingered at the

back of the kitchen, near the door that led to the backyard. "You," she said. "You got in touch with Admiral Best."

Dr. Caron nodded. "I did. And before anyone gets bent out of shape about that, I didn't tell him where we are in the Brava System. I only told him that he needed to get a grip on illegal research and that a water company was after my daughter and her friends, and if anything happened to her, I would personally cut him apart, piece by piece, without bothering to sedate him."

Dasha had never heard such vitriol in her father's voice, and it made her shiver.

"I told him to issue a galaxy-wide order to leave all of you the hell alone," Dr. Caron continued. "It didn't happen as quickly as it should have, but Best still made it happen. And I hope after that contact that I will never have to speak to him again."

"Getting a message from him was certainly a surprise," Lukas said flatly. "I'm even more surprised that he offered to help."

"But you're safe now," Dr. Caron said. "All of you. It was made very clear that you're to be left alone, although I don't think any of you can ever go back to the Zone."

"I don't think any of us want to," Jason said, speaking for the first time. He rolled his shoulders and winced. "Fucking EMP. It's hell on the muscles." He looked at Esme and Adam. "Sorry, I forgot about Rosie."

"I don't think she was listening," Esme replied.

"You have to support his head like this," Matthias said from the living room. "There, now you have it. Let me know when your arm gets tired."

Esme touched Serena's shoulder. "Are you okay with my kid holding your newborn?"

Serena thought for a second. "Matthias is there," she said. "Sullivan's fine. It's cute that Rosie's so fascinated with him."

Dasha steered the conversation back to her father. "Dad, I need to talk to you for a minute," she said. She crossed the room and held open the door.

Rordan motioned to follow her, but she shook her head. "I'll be back in a bit," she promised.

She and Dr. Caron stepped into the backyard. A light rain misted them, and, from the barn, Dolly the goat bleated. They walked along the grass in no particular direction.

"Thank you for doing that," Dasha said once they were away from the house. "You've saved all their lives."

"I played a big part in ruining them in the first place. It was the least I could do." Dr. Caron smoothed a few locks of silver hair against his scalp. "I will never forgive the admiral for what he did with my technology and to his own son, but I was in a position where I could finally do something about it. I hope I made some things right today."

Dasha stopped in her tracks. Dr. Caron did likewise.

"I need you to believe me when I say that Rordan didn't kidnap me or coerce me to leave with him," she said. "And I need you to forgive him someday."

A muscle ticked in her father's jaw. "That's going to be hard to do."

"I'm asking you to please work on it," she said. "For me." She steeled herself for what she was about to say. "I love him. And he loves me, too."

The rain shifted from a mist to a drizzle, as if to illustrate her point. Or her father's rage toward Rordan. She tucked a damp strand of hair behind her ear and waited for his response.

"Do you think he's capable of not being a jackass who will induce heart failure in me?" he finally asked.

That was promising. "Yes."

Dr. Caron noisily exhaled. "I'm not going to pretend I'm

thrilled about this," he said. "But if he loves you and cares about you, I'll support both of you."

"I know it was fast," Dasha said. "But sometimes you just know."

"Your mother and I married six months after we met, so yes, I understand that sometimes you do." In the light offered by the stars, Dasha could see a sad wistfulness in her father's eyes as he remembered her mother.

"And now that we don't have a water company after us, I want to go back to Sidra Prime," she said. "I love everyone here, but it isn't my home."

"That's your decision to make," Dr. Caron replied. "I'm going to stay for the time being, but if you want to go home, it's waiting for you."

"And I'm taking Rordan with me."

"I assumed you would."

They started walking back to the house. "Are you upset?" Dasha asked.

"Now that you're safe, no," Dr. Caron replied. "You're my daughter, and I love you. I want you to be happy. If making a life with Rordan Alexander will do that, then I want it for you, too."

Cecily met them at the door. "Remember the bounty hunter you fired on?"

"You didn't mention you fired on a bounty hunter!" Dr. Caron exclaimed.

Dasha realized she hadn't told her father the whole story since they returned to Kurkay-2. "Yeah," she said. "But remember that we're okay."

Cecily continued as they walked back into the kitchen. "Anyway, the *Rook* was disabled for a couple of hours, during which the admiral's cyborg statement was broadcast. Once the military received that order, they had to arrest the bounty hunter piloting it. The admiral just contacted Lukas again with the news."

"And Wilton's been taken over," Lukas added. "I think it's really over."

"Not yet," said Dr. Caron. With stern looks at Dasha and Rordan in turn, he said, "You're going to tell me what happened on Spaceport 44. This black market surgeon, the bounty hunter, *everything*."

Dasha took a seat at the table. She and Rordan exchanged a quick, knowing look. They'd be telling her father *almost* everything.

"Well," Rordan began. "The surgeon was a former military nurse and a friend of my family..."

DASHA LOOKED like she was ready to cry tears of joy once the passenger shuttle landed on Princess Cay. She threaded her fingers through Rordan's as they stepped through the airlock into bright sunshine and humid air. "I missed this so much," she said.

Rordan was surprised by the tropical heat. Garshan's climate was warm and mild, but never hot like this. He liked it.

They rented a flitter to take them to the home Dr. Caron and Dasha had shared. It was constructed in and around a massive tree, a sign outside proclaiming its name as "Sanctuary." The home was one of several such treehouses, and once inside, Rordan could see a wide, sandy beach below, full of people.

"Everything's as it should be," Dasha said as she inspected the home. She threw herself on the couch. "It feels so good to be home."

Rordan sat next to her and reached for her foot, massaging it. "Oh, hey," she said. "Don't stop that, please."

He continued for a couple of minutes until she said, "We did the right thing coming here, didn't we?"

"Now that it's safe for us to split up, yes," he replied. "And we won't be alone for that long."

Dr. Caron planned to return to Sidra Prime and the Princess Cay treehouse in a few months when Sullivan was older. Cecily and Jason would also be arriving in a few days, to take a look at properties for sale nearby. Dasha and Rordan were looking forward to having them as neighbors.

There was also the matter of finding a place of their own at some point, but neither of them was in a rush to do so right away.

"I'm still going to miss everyone," Dasha said. "Kurkay-2 wasn't my home so much as our friends there." She sighed.

"We aren't the only ones leaving," Rordan reminded her.

It wasn't only Cecily and Jason looking to relocate. When Sullivan was older, Matthias had every intention of returning to his work as an independent freighter operator aboard his ship, the *Ensign*, with Serena and the baby at his side.

But Valenna and Anders were staying on their homestead. Lukas and Cressida would be joining them in the farming operations, giving up their Westingtown apartment for a separate house they were building on the property. Adam was staying, too, and had joined one of the construction crews that was building Westingtown from the ground up. Esme was planning on opening a childcare center for the growing children's population in town.

His surviving cyborg brothers-in-arms were thriving, himself included. They'd made it through hell and survived.

Relief and gratitude brought tears to his eyes. *Praise be to the stars and universe, for giving me more chances at starting my life over.*

"Rordan? Are you all right?" Dasha regarded him curiously from the other end of the couch.

"I'm very all right," he said. "I love you, and I'm going to tell you that every day for the rest of our lives."

"I love you, too," she said, her own eyes suspiciously bright. She sat up and reached for his hand, a knowing smile on her face. "Come on, let me show you my bedroom."

He followed her through the house, secure in the knowledge that he was finally home.

ABOUT THE AUTHOR

Jessica Marting is a sci-fi and paranormal romance author, art enthusiast (not quite an artist, despite all that time in art school), an avid reader, and makeup collector. She lives in Toronto.

Sign up for her newsletter at jessicamarting.com/newsletter for pre-order alerts, sales, freebies, and more.

ALSO BY JESSICA MARTING

Magic & Mechanicals

Wolf's Lady

Sea Change

Bound in Blood

Dragon's Keep

Zone Cyborgs

Haven

Paradise

Oasis

Safe Harbor

Sanctuary

Refuge

The Commons

Supernova

Celestial Chaos

Standalone Novels & Novellas

Spindle's End

Trade Secrets

Neon Vice

Dead Ringer

Escape From Europa 10

Castaways

Demon's Favor

9 781989 780183